I0590631

RESCUED BY THE BERSERKER

A WARRIOR ROMANCE

LEE SAVINO

FREE BOOK

Get a secret Berserker book, Bred by the Berserkers (only to the awesomesauce fans on Lee's email list)
Go here to get started... https://geni.us/BredBerserker

RESCUED BY THE BERSERKER

A short, steamy, standalone shifter romance starring a huge, dominant warrior and the female he claims for his own.

Knut:

I'm a Berserker warrior, one of the best in the pack. So when the Alphas send me on a mission, nothing will stop me from tracking our enemies down and bringing them to justice.

Then Hazel runs across my path...

A flower in the wilderness, she is young, and fragile, and afraid. She's on the run from an evil mage who wants her power for his own.

She's mine. She just doesn't know it yet.

***

The Berserker Saga

Berserker Brides

KNUT

"I do not like this place." Leif stood at my side, axe raised, ready to strike an unseen enemy.

I grunted in agreement and frowned at the wilderness, a tangle of overgrown brush and briars. The forest had given way to sandy soil and the few trees were twisted and malformed, their showing roots bleached white.

"There is something wrong with the air," the redheaded warrior continued. "I do not wish to linger."

"Nor do I," I told him. "But we press on until we find the traitors." We'd been tracking three wolves who'd stolen from the pack. The thieves had led us on a merry chase for the past few days and nights and we were tired, travel worn, with fraying tempers.

The wind rattled the trees, a sound like clinking bones.

"What is that scent on the breeze?" Leif raised his head and sniffed. I did the same and we both nearly gagged.

"Something died." I coughed.

"Corpses," Leif agreed. "Rotting meat. No wonder the thieves hid here. No one would go near this place, if they could help it."

"Let's push on." I motioned to the rest of the warriors—a band of twenty men, all heavily armed.

"Listen…" Brokk, a brown-haired brute of a warrior, raised a finger, "do you hear that?"

After a pause, we all heard it as well as he.

"Silence," Leif said. "No birds."

"Rolf has news," Brokk nodded to a large, grey wolf trotting towards us. It leapt onto a boulder to address us.

I've scouted ahead, the wolf reported, speaking via the pack bonds into our minds. *There is a rocky clearing near the foot of a hill where many draugr are milling about.*

"Draugr?" Leif frowned. "I have not heard that word since we left the Northlands."

Rolf shared an image of the draugr with us—thin men with greyish skin and expressionless faces.

They stink. The wolf sneezed. *There are many of them and they seem to be guarding a cave. I sense powerful, tainted magic.*

"Whatever witch or warlock created these beings, it must make its home inside the cave," Leif guessed.

"Such an evil should be obliterated," another warrior murmured and a few others agreed.

"What do we do, Knut?" Leif asked. "The Alphas expect us to find the thieves."

I weighed my answer. In the Alpha's absence, it was my decision. A part of me screamed to rush into battle, but I would not. I valued the lives of these men and counted them my friends, though I was careful not to let my guard down around them.

The traitors are close, Rolf said. *I caught their scent in the woods before I came upon the stinking creatures around the cave.*

"We continue our quest," I said. "If our path crosses these creatures, we will fight. Until then, we stay on the trail of the three traitors."

We can stay in the forest and go around the cave, avoiding these draugr.

Motioning to the wolf, I let Rolf lead the way. The rest of the pack followed hard on my heels. We stalked with the stealth of wolves, fanning out in the forest, using our mind link to keep going in the right direction. Our path took us close to the sandy clearing Rolf had seen. Beyond a thin screen of trees were hundreds of sallow faced men, bodies shrunken to almost skin and bone. Whatever mage animated these beings, it did not keep its servants healthy. The men looked like walking corpses. Perhaps they were.

That explains the stink. Leif came to my side, his eyes glowing with an unnatural light. A signal that his beast was close to the surface, ready to break free.

I touched the redhead's arm and motioned for him to follow me back into the thick woods where there was no chance of the walking corpses sensing us watching them.

We could kill them all, Leif observed. *It might take days, but we could do it.*

We do not know this threat. It is not wise to provoke a fight.

Is the great warrior Knut running from a battle?

I glared at him and he stared back, meeting my gaze for a long second before dropping it in admission to my authority as the stronger wolf.

I am not a coward, Leif. Challenge me again, and I'll prove my dominance. But first let us find the thieves and return them to the Alphas for punishment.

Leif jerked his head in agreement. I let his insolence slide. Tensions were high and the enemy was close. Situations like these tested the hierarchy of the pack. If we returned home alive and he still wanted to fight, I'd indulge him.

We picked up our pace to catch up with rest of the warriors.

I lost the trail, Rolf whined. The wolf ran along with his nose close to the ground, stopping to sneeze at intervals. *Damned stinking draugr.*

I can help him, Leif barely looked to me for permission before setting aside his weapons and starting to strip off his clothes.

"Wait," I said aloud before Leif could complete the Change to wolf. "We do not know if the corpse beings sense magic."

Leif growled in answer. He didn't care. He wanted to provoke the beings, wanted to fight.

Normally I'd agree. But not today. Too much was at stake.

"We need to focus," I said. "The three thieves led us here. Why?"

"They wanted the stench of those beings to throw us off the trail," another warrior, a broad-shouldered Viking named Thorbjorn, guessed.

"But they have in their keeping the most precious treasure to the pack. They would not risk getting so close to evil." I shook my head.

Knut's right, Rolf said. *The thieves will not want to stay in this place. Perhaps they came on it by accident and now are trying to avoid us and the evil.*

"Why do we stand here talking when we could be killing things?" Leif's voice was more guttural.

"It's not like you to be itching for a fight," I said to Leif. The proximity of the enemy was provoking the redhead's temper.

"It's not like you to be running from one," he spat back.

I snarled at him.

My body itched, ready for the Change. I resisted. If I gave in to my magic now, with a large threat so near, I would not shift into the form of the wolf, but my third form, the beast. The beast was powerful, but dangerous. A weapon of last resort.

Control yourself, my order cracked like a whip through the pack bonds and every warrior straightened.

"The evil magic is affecting us," I spoke out loud to the pack. "We must leave here, before it provokes Berserker rage." Leif's chest rose and fell, but he'd pulled on his boots and reclaimed his weapons.

Apologies, Knut, he spoke to me privately. The glow in his eyes faded as he regained his grip on the beast.

I found the trail, Rolf told us.

"Onward," I ordered.

We'd gone no further than a few steps, when something crashed in the forest ahead of us. I threw out my hand to stop Leif from barging forward. The whole pack breathed down my neck as they halted.

Something's coming this way. Leif tensed, his hand over his nose, anticipating the rotting stench.

I sniffed the air and blinked. Instead of the corpse smell, a light, floral scent filled my nose.

Following it, I walked forward, my axe and shield drooping towards the ground.

"Knut," Leif called to me, "What are you doing? You could be walking into a trap."

I barely heard him; more than anything I wanted to fling my weapons aside and run to the source of the beautiful smell. My muscles tightened. I needed to run. I needed to hunt. My cock twitched in my pants. I needed to mate.

The sweet smell mingled with the rotten wind and I snorted, coming out of my daze.

"Knut? What is it?" Brokk asked.

"Something's out there..." I answered. "And not one of the corpses. Something still alive."

"Want me to scout it out?" Leif offered.

I grunted. We needed to know what danger we were walking into. But I wanted to go alone, to see if I could find and claim the sweet-smelling prize.

"Wait here," I said and started forward. I'd gone only two steps before a small form crashed through the bushes in front of us and skidded to a stop. The figure was short, smooth-limbed, with a pleasing face and hair of burnished chestnut. The young woman shrieked when she saw us, throwing up her hands—she held some sort of stick—and ran back the way she came.

HAZEL

I raced as fast as my legs would carry me. Behind me the gruesome creatures, servants of the Corpse King, came lurching after me.

I might be able to outrun them, but they had more than speed as a weapon.

My head throbbed, the lingering results of the spell they'd cast on me. *Tired. Cold. Can't get away.* The spell worked like an invisible net, slowing me. My legs turned as sluggish as my mind.

Please, I prayed to the goddess. *Please.* My left hand clutched the piece of witch's staff to my heart, willing it to aid me.

As I reached the forest edge, I put on a burst of speed, and ran through the brush—straight into the path of a group of warriors.

The men froze, staring at me. I screamed. Grey Men chasing me and warriors blocking my path. The big one in front, a burly blond with a large, wicked axe, stepped forward.

I darted away, branches whipping my calves. My breath sobbed in my throat as I fled, now praying that those men would not follow.

KNUT

Broken branches swayed in the wake of the woman. The warriors all spoke at once. *Who was that? A woman! Was that what you scented?* A few wanted to Change into wolves, whining with eagerness to run and hunt.

"Hold," I shouted. "The enemy lies ahead."

The pack strained at my command, but as the most dominant wolf, I held them with my power.

My own beast roared to life, fighting for control. The woman had been barefoot, frightened, wearing no more than a thin white garment—a simple shift that she might wear to sleep. She should not be out in the wilderness, anywhere near the disgusting draugr. She needed help.

She needed me.

"She smells of strawberries," Leif said in awe. Of all the wolves, he was almost strong enough to break my commands. In a daze, he made to move forward and I whirled with a growl.

"No. This prey is mine."

HAZEL

My change of direction took me back out of the forest, into the Grey Men's path. I veered again, finding shelter in a knot of scrub pine on the edge of the great sandy clearing, much too close to the cave I'd escaped from for comfort. I dropped down behind a boulder to catch my breath.

I did not know where to go, where to run. The Grey Men were everywhere. They'd followed me since I escaped from the cave where their master—the Corpse King, a sorcerer with enough power to make these awful creatures his servants—slept in a spelled state.

The Corpse King had drained my friend, Sari, of all her blood. If I hadn't escaped, I was going to be next.

A hissing noise told me the Grey Men were nearing my hiding place. I crouched, trembling. I had a stick in my hand —a piece of a witch's staff that had magically come to my aid, but no weapons. My life at the abbey, working at the looms with the other orphans and tending the garden, tanned my limbs and strengthened them, but had not prepared me to defend my life.

I gripped the carven wood tighter, ready for the final struggle. The Grey Men wouldn't drag me back to the Corpse King without a fight.

At least the headache the creatures cursed me with was gone. It had vanished the instant I laid eyes on the giant warrior leading the group of men in the woods. His brow had creased when he saw me, his whole body straining to run after me, even as he raised a hand to make his men stay back. Whatever made my feet want to run to him and hide in the shelter of his arms, I know he felt it too.

Beyond the boulder, a hissing noise heralded the Grey Men's approach. They were searching for me, combing the sandy area and would soon come upon my hiding place.

A shadow fell across me as I rose to run. I whirled to face the threat.

The blond warrior loomed over me. My heart stopped as I looked up, craning my neck as far as it would go. Large as an oak, his taut muscle stretched his leather jerkin and breeches. He still held his great axe and shield, yet his footfalls were as light and silent as a predator's.

He stalked closer and I let out a squeak.

"What are you doing here, little rabbit?" His eyes pierced me, hot and golden.

I backed away, edging around the boulder. At this moment, the warrior was more of a threat than the Grey Men.

He laid down his weapon, hand outstretched as he approached. "Easy, easy," he almost purred. The sound soothed the tension from my spine. "We must go from this place, lass. You are not safe."

His large hand, rough and scarred, reached for me. Another step and he'd have me in his grasp.

I panicked, staggering back. "No."

"Stop," he snapped and my knees almost buckled at the command. He had some sort of power over me—I wanted to do exactly as he said. But I was done taking orders from men.

He lunged for me and I darted out of reach—right into the cold, dead hands of the Grey Men.

KNUT

A snarl broke from my chest as my woman ran straight into the enemy's clutches. The draugr hissed in triumph, grey fingers latching onto her lovely arms with a bruising grip, dragging her back, away from me.

She cried out and my vision went red.

I caught up my axe and I charged.

The creatures gave me a blank look of surprise, right before I lopped off their heads. The horrible hissing noise stopped as the blade cleaved their necks, as easily as snapping dead blooms from a flower. Fluid burst from their necks as they fell. I staggered back at the stench.

The woman screamed again, now covered in gore, and fought away from the dead men's grip. The headless bodies still clutched at her, until I slammed them with my shield and followed it with a kick to get them to release my woman.

Bony fingers caught my arms, pulling me back, and I roared, throwing the draugr off me. The corpse beings had skin clammy to the touch and smelled even worse when their bodies split open. Their rotten flesh wouldn't tempt a starving wolf.

Corpses piled at my feet, I howled in triumph. This would be a battle for the bards to sing my praises.

"Look out," the woman shrieked. I whirled just in time to duck a sword. The rusty blade swooped over my head. I charged. The sword swiped at me again and this time I caught it in my bare hand, and wrenched it out of the draugr's grip before wading in for the kill. I'd lost my shield, but my axe made short work of chopping the draugr into a greyish pile of limbs.

A small gasp made me turn.

The woman stood staring at me, holding the piece of wood to her chest like a babe. She'd shouted to save me. She didn't know that Berserkers felt nothing in the heat of battle —not pain, not fear.

More Grey Men were closing in as I grabbed her wrist, tugging her forward. "Come on. We must run."

She looked at my hand in horror. Blood dripped from my palm, but the wound had already started to close— Berserker healing at work. But that wasn't why she was distressed.

My arm had sprouted fur, and my fingers ended in sharp claws—the start of the Change into the beast.

I pulled her to me and she fought, kicking, until I tossed her over my shoulders.

Steadying her with one hand, I gripped my axe with the other and ran.

HAZEL

The wind knocked out of me, I couldn't shout. Hands braced on the warrior's back, I raised my head enough to see the Grey Men slithering after us. The warrior plunged into the forest, moving faster than was humanly possible.

He'd caught the blade in his hand. He'd destroyed the Corpse King's servants with inhuman strength and speed, and for a moment, I'd caught a glimpse of the beast-like form underneath his human one, the monster waiting to break free.

Whoever my captor was, he was more than a man.

As my breath returned to me, I started to struggle. I still held the piece of the witch's staff—my left hand clutched it so hard I may never pry it free. I knocked the warrior's legs with it and his hand clapped my bottom.

"Stop that," the warrior grunted.

He plunged into a stream and waded forward. When he reached a deeper pool, he swung me down. I yelped, thrashing in the freezing water.

He caught me in his brutally strong arms, an arm around my waist and hand over my mouth.

"Be silent," he rasped into my ear. "We must wash the living corpse's scent from our bodies. This way, they cannot track us."

My teeth knocked together under his palm sealing my lips, but I relaxed.

"Good girl," he murmured. "It's going to be all right. I'll not let them take you."

My legs were almost numb before he swooped me up in his arms and waded out of the pool. The freezing water didn't seem to affect him.

Too cold and shocked to cry out, I clung to him, a source of heat if nothing else. I could struggle and scream, but no one besides the Grey Men would hear me. Whatever this warrior was, I was stuck with him until I could escape.

Desperate to get warm, I pressed my face to the warm flesh at the base of his throat, just above the collar of his jerkin. My body shook against his massive chest.

The warrior strode through the woods, carrying me as if I weighed no more than dandelion fluff.

"What were those things?" he murmured.

"I don't know," my teeth chattered as I answered. "They brought me into the cave so their master could drain me of blood."

A growl rumbled under my ear, but it wasn't directed at me. He pulled me in closer.

"Did you see the mage that made them?"

"The Corpse King. Yes, I saw him." He had looked like a corpse, wrapped in grave clothes, lying on a stone slab with his armor nearby, ready for when he would rise again and lead a conquering army of his Grey Men. "He still sleeps. The servants brought us there as a sacrifice to set him free."

"Us? They captured more than one of you?" Abruptly, the warrior changed course, darting faster between the giant trees.

"Yes." I didn't know why I was telling him this, or why I felt so safe in his arms. I didn't even know his name. "There was another young woman with me, named Fleur. Please, you must help her."

The warrior cursed and broke into a run that had the landscape blurring around us.

I slipped an arm around his shoulders to hang on tighter. He wore a slight frown as he wove through the trees. If I met him in a village market, I would think he was a flesh and blood man, a hardened soldier, mercenary even, but one who followed a code of honor. Maybe I could trust him.

You can. His voice spoke right into my head. Another sign I was hallucinating. The warrior wasn't even looking at me, but ahead at the trail.

Gripping the staff, I did the same and shrieked as a giant wolf bounded into our path.

"Hush, lass, 'tis only Rolf." The warrior carrying me stopped dead in his tracks and spoke to the wolf. "But where are the others?"

"Knut," two warriors appeared, bursting from the trees. One brown haired with thick black brows, the other a redhead. "We got separated when a party of *draugr* attacked. Who is this woman?" They gaped at me.

"Never mind," Knut told them. "The thieves we sought —they lost their quarry. The spaewife Fleur is in the cave with the sleeping mage who made those Grey things."

"Grey Men," I corrected softly, and he heard me.

"Rally the pack to attack these draugr, these Grey Men," Knut ordered.

"What are you going to do?"

"Get this one to safety." His arms tightened around me.

"You defy the Alpha's orders?" This from a brown-haired, frowning warrior. "You were to lead us to hunt the traitors."

Knut's answer was a low growl.

The brown-haired warrior raised his hands and backed away. He and the wolf trotted off, but the red-haired one paused. "Who is she?"

Knut's answering growl sent tingles up and down my spine.

"She is mine."

KNUT

As Leif, Brokk and Rolf raced back towards the fray, I set a course for the west. The mountain where my pack made its home was many leagues from this evil, stinking place. My woman would not be safe until she was there with me, protected by the entire pack, living in the shelter I built for her and marked as my own.

She was mine, as I claimed, though she did not know it yet.

"My warriors will go back. They will save your friend. She is one of our pack and was taken from us several days ago. We have been searching for her and the trail led us to you."

An unforeseen treasure. A gift from the goddess I will not ever give up. I, Knut, a warrior to the bitter end, disobeying my leader's mandate. I would rescue her, and accept my Alpha's punishment.

We reached the river again and she struggled. "Put me down. I want to walk."

I held her fast. "We will travel faster if I carry you. Besides, you have no shoes."

"I do not know you," she pressed her hands against my chest. "I do not want to go with you."

I saw red again, and fought for control. To wait so long for the woman to break the curse, only to succumb to it now--it would not be born. I had to rein in the beast.

"Stop, little one. You are not thinking clearly. You are in shock," I growled.

She struggled further and I threw her over my shoulder, peppering her soft backside with a few decisive smacks.

The beast inside me surged to the fore. It wanted to mark her, tear her flesh, taste her blood, give a wound that would scar and show all she was in my possession.

I gritted my teeth, resisting the call to turn into a monster.

A sharp pain blossomed in my backside. I howled and swung her back down. She backed away, still holding the splintered end of the stick she'd stabbed me with.

"None of that." I charged, easily snatching the piece of carved wood away. I tossed it aside. In a flash, I was in front of her, dropping to one knee and tugging her over it. Her hands hit the ground as my palm connected with her sweet bottom. Her butt cheeks wobbled under the thin fabric. I bared her bottom and turned pink with a few well-placed swats. The beast within in me crowed its savage approval, but I was calm and levelheaded.

She had to obey, so I could keep her safe.

My woman didn't cry, but let out little angry grunts as I punished her. I did not like disciplining her so soon, but she needed to know who was in charge and this was the fastest way to teach her.

Four more heavy swats and I clamped a hand on the back of her neck, holding her still. My other cupped her glowing cheeks.

"Now, will you listen to me?"

She kicked in response and I let loose on her bottom, a series of forceful smacks to show her I would not tolerate her resistance. After a minute, her frustrated sounds turned to breathless mews. I smacked the tops of her thighs a few times and added one or two to the apex of her legs.

A gasp and a sweet tang filled the air, mingling with her strawberry scent. Arousal.

But I wasn't the only one who scented it.

The woods around us filled with a sibilant sound, coming closer. Grey Men. We'd lingered too long.

"Be still." I clasped her in my arms. "Our enemies are near."

My woman had a dazed expression. Not frightened or upset, but docile. "We will escape this," I told her. "But you will follow my commands. Understand?"

She had enough presence of mind to nod. Her face was flushed, an after effect of her hanging head down over my bent knee, but also a sign of her excitement. She'd responded to the impromptu discipline. She lay a hand against my jaw, steadying herself.

I stole a quick kiss, just a hard press of my lips against hers. A touch of heaven, in case the next fight was my last. "I won't let them take you," I promised and pulled her up. She clung to my hand with both hers.

The hissing came from three sides now.

"They are trying to surround us." I backed up, taking her with me. "When I tell you to run, you run."

If she escaped now, I could keep the Grey Men from her and track her later. Perhaps she wouldn't see the beast come over me, shaping my form into a magical creature twice as tall as her, with fur and claws—a vicious blend of human and wolf. "Now." I pushed her. My voice was a guttural bark as my throat reshaped. Magic tingled at the base of my spine, my bones ready to crack and shift with the Change. "Go," I grunted.

When the Grey Men came through the trees at me, she ran to pick up the splintered staff, and whirled with me to face the enemy as if the stick was a sword.

When I gestured to her to flee, she gripped her meager weapon tighter and shook her head.

Fur was already rippling down my arms when I scooped up my woman and dropped her at the base of an oak.

"Stay," I told her. I wished I could protect her from the sight of the monster I would become, but the spanking hadn't touched her stubbornness. If I wasn't so annoyed, I'd almost be proud.

Whirling with a roar, I attacked the creatures before the first wave could reach her. I'd left my shield but still had my axe, sent it crashing into the frontrunner of the ranks of corpse-like creatures, and completed the Change. Rage turned my vision red. Shouting my battle cry, I charged, unafraid. I was suffering under a greater curse than these draugr and capable of far more evil.

I would save my woman even it if earned me her fear.

HAZEL

The monster fought the Grey Men while I cringed against a tree. The transformed warrior had black fur, a giant's height, inhuman speed, and a heavy muzzle. A tawny fringe along its spine was the only thing it shared with the blond man. That and its fighting abilities.

When the dust settled pieces of Grey Men littered the area. I screamed as a severed arm wriggled towards me and the hand tried to grab my ankle. I tried kicking it away, but it hung on tight until I touched the staff to it. The wood tingled in my hand and the disembodied arm flew off as if lightning had struck it, flopping into the path of the monster. Lethal jaws snapped at it, swallowing it down.

And vomited it back up.

Nasty. It spat, several times. *Not good to eat.* The voice in my head had a rough quality, closer to a bark than human words.

The monster stood on its hind legs, straightening until it was at least twice as tall as me. It's form was vaguely man like, with a chest and arms of banded muscle, all covered with black fur.

My breath shuddered through me. I'd seen many horrible things this day, in the lair of the sorcerer, but this beast was the stuff of nightmares.

It bellowed its triumph, and swiveled its head towards me.

Come. Somehow it spoke right into my mind.

"No," I whispered. As it stalked my way, I scuttled backwards, trying to get my feet under me to run. With the Grey Men dispatched, I had my chance to escape this monster.

It stopped and cocked its head. Grunted as if trying to speak.

I turned and crawled away, only to have a clawed hand grab the scruff of my neck. With a cry, I turned and stabbed it with the staff. The monster bellowed and dropped me in surprise.

Finding my feet, I pushed through the thicket and when it came after me, I let the branches I held snap back into its face.

KNUT

Frightened, annoying little rabbit. So delectable, the plump, tanned legs flashing under her short garment, the curvy chest heaving as she ran from me. I stalked her easily, ready at any moment to speed up and complete the chase. The beast was ready to rut, but I was still in control. Her scent called me out of the rage and into my right mind. Not even mated yet, and the curse was already lifting.

But she was afraid of me. I had just slain her enemies—the corpse blood vile on my tongue—but she'd almost rather face the Grey Men than me.

How is your rescue going? Leif asked, and shared with me an image of his own battle with the draugr. He and the rest of the pack had found the traitors and Fleur, the woman they'd stolen, at the mouth of the mage's cave, hard-pressed by the stinking Grey Men.

She stabbed me with her stick. Twice. I sent the picture of her standing with the staff, her face a mask of fear, and her body still ready to fight.

And you let her? Leif laughed. I was not close to any of my fellow warriors, preferring to stand apart, but Leif ignored my distance.

I don't want to hurt her. Of course, now that she was running, she might hurt herself. Emotion prickled in my chest, something I hadn't felt in sometime. Fear.

This little female woke all sorts of new things inside me.

I hear that is the way when you find your true mate. Leif's thought was tinged with jealousy and wonder. Shocked I'd shared so much through the bond, I stayed silent. I was a leader among the pack, but usually kept apart from the rest of the men.

She must be special, if you are breaking orders to go after her. Take care, Knut. Whatever these creatures are, something controls them, and has power enough to cast spells.

Above my head, the sky was boiling with clouds. A storm was coming, howling up from the east. No doubt its origin was the mage's cave.

I will rescue this woman and see what she knows. I will bring her back to the mountain for the Alphas to question. They might forgive me for abandoning my post if I brought them a better quarry. *To the fight and the finish!*

To the fight and the finish! The warrior responded with a roar.

With my own shout, I charged and broke through the branches the little one had pushed through in an attempt to stop me in my tracks. She would learn that it wasn't so easy to best a Berserker.

HAZEL

T he wind whipped faster, the trees tossed their
heads. My hair stood on end. Something was
happening and even the weather responded.

I broke through the trees and stopped at the mad scene
before me. My wild escape had lead me back to the cave of
the Corpse King.

My friend Fleur was in the midst of the battle, armed
with the second half of the staff I held. A warrior, a wolf, and
an eagle fought beside her, pressing their way to escape into
the wood.

Everywhere giant warriors fought the Grey Men like
mad things. Half men, half monsters, the crashed into the
enemy, catching the blades in their bare hands and driving
the Corpse King's servants back with violent glee.

A fine sight to see, isn't it not?

I whirled. There was no one behind me, yet a voice, a
deep and tender male voice, had spoken in my head. But
that was impossible. I still held the staff. Perhaps it was
playing tricks on me.

More Grey Men were rushing into the fray, coming from every direction. I would not be safe for long.

I backed away, right into a broad, bare chest. The blond warrior who'd fought for me in monstrous form loomed over me with a determined expression. He had scratches on his face from where I'd let the branches slash him.

"Got you now," he grunted and tossed me over his shoulder to carry me off—again.

KNUT

W ith the wriggling woman over my shoulder, I strode off. She was struggling and fighting. I enjoyed the soft, pleasant feel of her body against mine.

I put a warning hand on her bottom. "Stab me again with that damn twig, and I'll roast your bum right here. See if I don't." The threat made her still.

Behind us rose the clang of weapons and roars of the Berserkers facing their enemies. The draugr were everywhere, an endless stinking sea.

Leif, Rolf, I called as reinforcements swarmed near us. *More vermin. Help me clear a path.*

Holding the woman with one hand, I cut through the ranks with my axe. A storm had blown up overhead and a thick mist was pouring from the cave's mouth.

The mage had woken and was fighting back.

Swiping at enemies as they popped out of the unearthly fog, I kept a mindlink with the woman I carried. A bond had opened between us, as sure and true as the bond I shared with the rest of the pack. The woman's thoughts were jumbled and frightened and, as the fog increased, a heavy sadness settled over her, a sickness of the mind.

Dismayed, I darted into the woods and shrugged her down into my arms. Her face was deathly pale.

Cold. No escape. Despair.

"Wake up, lass," I cupped her cheeks. "It's a curse, only a curse. The mage is working his evil magic through this fog."

But she didn't respond. Whether from fear or exhaustion, she'd fainted.

A rumbling started at the base of the hill. The earthquake threw Grey Men to the ground, which was covered in thick layer of fog.

The cave is collapsing-retreat! The Alpha's order rang through the pack bonds, a powerful compulsion that my Berserker brothers immediately obeyed. I resisted. As the ground began to shake with more violence, thick dust spewed from the cave. I threw myself down, covering the woman with my body until the worst was over. Cradling her in my arms, I ran the rest of the way to safety.

HAZEL

I woke to the sound of rushing water. Light drops bathed my face until the warm bulk under me shifted, moving me away from the wet spray. Soft fur rubbed my face, wiping it dry.

I opened my eyes. A few feet from me water fell in a thick, grey sheet, roaring past the crevice where I lay.

"You're awake."

A voice in the gloom made me shoot up to my feet. I staggered, slipping on the slick rocks between me and the waterfall. A hand clamped on my arm and pulled me back from the edge. Muscled arms closed around me.

"I would not move if I were you," the warrior half spoke, half growled in my ear. He moved us both back to safety before he let me go. With his height, he had to bend a little in the small space. His wet blond locks hung about his face and his skin bore faint scratches from the branches I'd sent whipping into his path, plus more cuts and blade marks that hadn't been there before.

He stayed still and quiet while I turned in a small circle, taking in the black, wet rock and the rushing water.

"What—where?" I stammered.

"We're in a cave behind a waterfall, some leagues away from the mage's cave and his servants. The enemy sent out a curse that touched your mind. You fainted and I carried you away." His large hand drifted over my hair, brushing back the wet strands sticking to my face. "You're safe here, with me."

I wrapped my arms around my body, but didn't retreat. His massive body was a source of welcome heat. He'd already rescued me several times and carried me in his arms to this hidden sanctuary. If he wanted to touch me now, I wouldn't protest.

Besides, unless I edged closer to the waterfall, there wasn't much space to run. The blond warrior seemed to take up every available inch with his hard-muscled body. He stood bare-chested in ripped breeches. When he turned, I gasped. A broken arrow stuck from his back, near his waist.

"You're hurt." I pointed to the thick bolt. He glanced down as if he hadn't seen it before. With a grunt, he pulled it from his flesh and tossed it into the raging fall of water a few feet from us.

Blood gushed from the wound. Without thinking, I went and pressed my hands against it, trying to stem the flow.

His large hand closed over mine.

"It's alright, lass. It'll heal soon enough."

"But—"

He lifted away my palm and showed me that the skin had already closed.

I jerked my hand away. "Who are you?" I asked in a shaky voice. "What are you?"

"Afraid, little one?"

I jerked my head yes, but realized it was a lie. After my

initial shock, I felt calm in his presence, as if, deep down, I knew I was safe with him.

A grin creased his features, barely discernible in the gloom. "That's right, little one. You have nothing to fear."

My forehead creased. Was he reading my mind?

He took my hand and drew me down to sit on the rocks.

"I am called Knut. I am a warrior."

"You're a man...but..." I searched for a way to describe the monster he'd become before my eyes.

Sadness touched his mouth. "I am a man and more than a man. Long ago a witch gave me and my fellow warriors great power. The magic had...consequences."

I shivered in the cool, damp air.

"Here." He lifted a large white pelt and laid it over my shoulders.

"We won't stay here long. You need warmth and care." He touched my knee, drawing my attention to the scratches there. My shift was filthy, my feet dirty and cut.

"Why are we in this place?"

"The Grey Men do not seem to like water."

"Are they here?" I half-started up in alarm.

"Easy," he pulled me into his arms. "I believe they are tracking you. I ran in the river to make sure they would lose the trail, but the mage bespelled the weather. We will wait out the storm and then I will sneak us out."

I huddled awkwardly in his lap, dwarfed by his broad body. My shoulders were hunched, but when he stroked my back, I naturally angled towards his muscled chest, allowing him to draw me further into his embrace.

Under my ear, his heart beat against the roar of the waterfall. Some light came in through the blue-grey sheet, enough for me to study the warrior's face. Tall and blond, like the Viking raiders most villages still feared, though their dragon-headed ships hadn't touched our shores for many years. His skin bore scars, his face lined with the weight of his years, yet he was handsome. Every word, every move spoke of authority. He was a man used to giving orders, and having them obeyed. Yet the way he looked at me...

My hands tugged on the pelt he'd tucked around my shoulders, drawing it tighter, but the fur was frail armor against the warrior's penetrating gaze. He was studying me as I was him, a small smile on those firm lips.

"Tell me your name," he said.

"Hazel," I answered, obeying before I decided whether telling him my name was folly. My name and the clothes on my back, were the only things left in my possession.

"And how old are you?"

"Eighteen summers, sir. At least, that's what the nuns at the abbey had told me. I was brought to the orphanage when I was a babe."

Knut's large hand came to cup my cheek. "So young to have such power over me." His voice rumbled through me as his gaze fixated on my lips.

"How old are you?" I dared not knock his arm away, even as my heart beat faster, responding to his touch. My breasts felt heavy, swollen. Something inside me shifted, waking up, like a flower blooming and turning towards the light.

He chuckled, and it took years off his face. "I do not know my age. I was born thirteen summers before I pledged allegiance to my jarl, twenty summers before the jarl sent me to fight to make Harald Fairhair king of the North Lands. A few summers after that, I was chosen to be part of an elite group of men, selected to become the greatest of all warriors. The witch cursed us and my life as a man ended and my life as a Berserker began."

A Berserker. I'd heard tales of such warriors, along with the stories of the Vikings who came to raid our shores. Warriors who feared nothing, shock troops that could destroy an entire army before their king sent the bulk of his forces into battle. Their inhuman violence and rage made them impervious to all harm. They'd fight until they dropped with exhaustion and nothing could stand in their way.

"I have not kept track of the years since then," he mused. "It has been many moons." He seemed more fascinated by my hair and weight on his lap, than telling me of his life. We were trapped behind the waterfall, with great danger lurking just outside, and yet he seemed content to have me sit in his lap, and examine every hair on my head with his worshipful gaze.

His great hand dropped to tug at mine, peeling my white-knuckled grip from the edge of the pelt. He studied my small fingers, my arm brown from days working in the sun.

Emboldened by the gentleness in his look and tone, I freed my hands and took his. Tingles spread through me as I stroked the fingers open, studied the scars and rough palms. The hands of a warrior.

Yet not long ago, they had been clawed and furred, a grotesque mix of human and wolf.

"Your hands, they were different when you were fighting the Grey Men." I tried to summon my repulsion, but I couldn't. "What are you?"

He set his finger against my lips and the simple touch sent warmth rushing through me. "Nothing you need fear."

I was trembling again, against my will. I steeled my spine. "Why are you helping me then?"

He cocked his head, tucked a strand of wet hair behind my ear. "I have been waiting for you a long, long time."

"I don't understand."

"You don't have to, little one. Some things are beyond understanding, but they are still true."

He tucked me under his chin. His bare chest emanated heat that seeped into my chilled body. At last, at long last, I could relax.

I closed my eyes. "I'm tired."

"Sleep, little one. I will keep watch."

I woke to him shaking me. "It's time to flee."

He drew me to my feet.

"Hazel, you must promise me to stay close and heed what I say."

My forehead wrinkled.

"The last time we faced these Grey Men, I ordered you to flee. Instead, you stood to face them and then ran from me. I understand you did not know who I was, but now you do. Disobey again and you'll face the consequences."

Anger made my cheeks flush. "Like a spanking?"

He lifted his chin. "Exactly."

Fists clenched at my side, I opened my mouth to argue and he caught my chin.

"You don't deny me. I am the only one standing between you and the Corpse King's creatures. You will heed my words and obey. If you don't it may mean your death and I will not tolerate that. Will you submit to me?"

There seemed to be only one answer the golden eyes would accept. "Yes." I had to work to wet my throat.

Immediately his hand on my chin gentled. "Poor little

one. So cold and all alone. You are not alone anymore. Do you understand?"

I just stared at him.

"Sweet rabbit," he murmured. But he dropped his hand and turned. "I am going to scout the way out of here. You will wait for my return."

I nodded. I had no desire to rush to face those Grey Men.

He moved to the cave entrance, light on his feet. I secured the pelt around my shoulders as best I could and picked up the piece of witch's staff. I did not understand what powers it had, but I was reluctant to leave it.

"Hazel," Knut called to me from the edge of the path behind the waterfall, his deep voice rumbling over the crashing sound. I hastened to his side.

"Good girl." He grinned down at me. I put my hand in his, clutching the short staff with the other, and he drew me back out into the light.

It was morning, soft sun just starting its arc through the sky. We'd spent the night together behind the falls.

"We have miles to go before we're beyond the Grey Men's reach. My friends have retreated back to our mountain home while the Alphas decide the best plan of attack. We have declared war on the Corpse King."

"And Fleur?" I asked.

"She is safe, home with the pack."

A little worry in me eased.

"Is that where you are taking me?"

"Yes," he said, glancing at the sky to determine our direction. "And no. I've lived in the barracks with the rest of the warriors, but will make a new home." He shot me a look I couldn't interpret. "The Alphas will allow me to build a lodge at the foot of the mountain for myself and my mate."

My heart twisted, but I kept my voice neutral. There was

no reason for me to be disappointed that this warrior was pledged to another. "You have a mate?"

This time I knew exactly what his grin meant. "I do now."

I nearly stumbled and he steadied me before pulling me along.

"Wait," I tugged on his hand. "What do you mean?"

"The moment I scented you on the wind, I knew you were mine."

I tried to free my hand, but he had an iron grip.

"Do not fight me on this, little one. We have enough enemies. We need not be at war with one another."

"I-I am not yours," I stammered.

"You are. But you have not realized it yet. Come. There is time to talk of this, when we are safe." Clasping my hand, he picked up the pace. He moved with the powerful grace of a predator, body tense on high alert for our enemies.

I trailed after him, wanting to stay close and wishing I could pull away. I had no choice but to follow him. There was nowhere else to go.

I'd spent my life sheltered in the abbey, trusting a caretaker who'd lied to me and the other orphans when he said he'd care for us. He'd sold me and Fleur, and who knows how many of my friends, to be fodder for the Corpse King.

Knut gave orders, but risked everything for my care. The more time I spent with him, the less I wanted to leave.

Which was ludicrous. He was attractive and capable, to be sure. But pledging myself to him forever, when we'd just learned each other's names?

As we made our way around a high hill, the wind shifted, bringing a rotting stench to our noses just as we ran into a group of Grey Men.

Knut tensed, pushing me behind him and drawing his

axe. We were in a deep ravine, with no way out but to run back.

Go, a voice sounded in my mind. Knut's. Impossible. I must be going mad.

I stepped back, hands twisting on the witch's staff. There were so many Grey Men and they were armed. They could overwhelm Knut while he was letting me escape.

"Run, Hazel," Knut ordered. "I will keep them from you." Before he finished speaking, the creatures closest to him attacked. Spears swung down and Knut faced them with a challenging roar.

Whirling, I began to run. A voice murmured in my head. *Head west and do not stop until you see mountains. I will call on the pack to come to your rescue, if I fall.*

I stopped. Biting my lip, I looked back. Knut's blond head bobbed amid the corpse-like creatures, ducking and wheeling as he fought many at once. If I left now, he would die.

In my hands, the wooden staff crackled with sudden energy.

A Grey Man had worked past Knut, trapping the Berserker between him and the rest of the horde. It slashed at Knut while he faced ten others.

My feet were moving before I could give it a thought.

The Grey Man raised a sword to stab at Knut's back—and jerked and stiffened when I thrust the staff at its back. Ripples ran through its body while it stood paralyzed. The sword fell from its lifeless fingers a second before it dropped.

Knut glanced back, incredulous.

"I told you to run," he grunted.

"Look out!" I screamed as two Grey Men leaped from the walls of the ravine, dropping onto the Berserker warrior.

With a cry, he tossed one off his back and threw the other into the advancing horde.

The creature landed near me and, before it could run and attack again, I whacked him with the staff. The Grey Man sizzled and he flew as if lightning had struck him. The smell of charred flesh filled the air and the rest of the Corpse King's servants hissed.

Under my fingers, the wood hummed. A second later, Knut's hand closed over mine and he pulled me along. We raced along the bottom of the ravine. My bare foot caught on a stone and I stumbled. Knut swung me up into his arms. I held onto his shoulders.

"The Grey Men—they're not following."

"Whatever magic is in that stick, it stunned them. I killed a few, but it did not deter them until you used that thing." He grimaced at the staff and I tucked it closer to my body, so it wasn't touching him. "Where did you get it?"

"A witch gave it to Fleur, before I met her. The friar broke it before the Grey Men took us from the abbey, but it appeared in the cave before I made my escape."

Knut grunted and I knew he didn't trust such magic.

He didn't stop running until he'd found the river again and crossed it. As the sun climbed higher, his pace slowed. We left the thick forest and came to a countryside of fields broken by a few copses.

Finally, he set me down.

"We're off course, but I do not want to lead the Grey Men back to the pack. We'll keep near water, for now."

He fed me dried meat and we both took bracing drinks from the river.

"We'll go this way," he said and caught my hand when I started forward. "You disobeyed me, little one."

"I saved your life," I retorted, then bit my lip, hoping he would not lose his temper.

He pressed his lips together. I heard his thought clearly in my mind.

First, we find safety. Then there will be a reckoning.

AS THE DAY WORE ON, the weather grew dark and strange. Grey clouds suffused the sun and a frightening voice carried on the wind, muttering in a language I could not understand.

"The Corpse King casting spells," Knut growled. "He seeks what he lost."

He lifted me again in his arms and increased our speed.

"I don't understand," I clung to the Viking and studied his features instead of watching the scenery pass by at a dizzying speed. "Why does he want me?"

"You are a spaewife."

"A what?"

"A woman with a special sort of magic, one that calls to the Corpse King."

I balked at this. "I have no magic."

"You do," the warrior said quietly. "For it calls to me, also. It quiets the beast."

I rubbed my face, wishing I could lie down and wake up back at the abbey. Even if it was a prison of sorts, it was safe. "I do not understand any of this. I am Hazel, named for a common herb. My own mother gave me up and I was raised as an orphan. I am nothing special."

"Your mother was probably a spaewife, also. Your ability comes through her." He held up a hand when I would protest. "You do have magic, otherwise the witch's staff would not be a weapon in your hands. Trust me, Hazel, you are no ordinary woman."

Too tired to argue further, I slept a little, head throbbing, shivering under the blackened sky.

I woke as Knut ducked into a low, dark dwelling.

"Where are we?" I thrashed as shadows covered us.

"Shhh," he set me down and kept his hands on my hips to steady me. "A crofter's farm. I checked and no one's about. You alright, lass?"

He waited for my nod to let me go. Numb, body trembling with fear and hunger, I watched him leave and return several times, fetching water, and wood to build a fire.

"The storm out there is nothing natural. We'll stay here until it passes," he told me.

"What happened to the people who lived here?" I asked. The hut had all the makings of a home lovingly built and then abandoned. There were dead flowers in a vase on the table, amid the cobwebs.

"This is the first farm we've found since leaving the Corpse King's cave. Nothing grows well in the presence of evil," Knut said. "As the mage's power grew, it may have touched this place. The crofters left before they starved." The wind gusted past the door, moaning with that eerie voice.

"Or went mad." I shuddered.

"No more talk of this." He stepped back from the blaze, dusting his hands. "Come to me, lass."

I scuttled closer to him and he placed me in front of the fire with my back to his bare chest. His large hands skimmed down my arms. "By the moon, you're freezing. Where is the pelt I gave you?"

"I lost it…"

"I will get you another." He hugged me. Between his large body and the fire, the chill ebbed from my bones.

I craned my head to look at him. "The wolf...is it one of your forms?"

"Yes." He paused for a long while as if reluctant to say more. "There are three. The wolf, the man, and the beast. You have seen the latter two."

Once I was warm, he went and found a blanket and shook it out, and laid it in front of the fire. I sat at his direction, setting the witch's staff aside and curling up with my chin on my knees. The fire crackled happily, a reassuring sound after the past two days filled with horrors. It was almost enough to make me forget what manner of warrior sat next to me.

Almost.

Knut crouched close, feeding the fire.

His hands were a normal man's, large and rough.

A witch's curse, he'd said.

"You fought well," I said, "against the Grey Men. Especially when you...turned into the beast."

He grunted and checked the pouch at his side for more dried meat, turned out a few strips, and pressed them into my hand. "I'll go hunting soon," he muttered.

I caught his hand and raised my voice so I would not be ignored. "This last time you fought, you were outnumbered. Why did you not turn into the beast?"

His shoulders rose and fell. At his silence, I knew I'd pushed too hard.

"Because, Hazel," he rose and towered over me. "Each time I allow the beast to take over, I lose a little more control. The beast will win out one day. Unless—" he paused, turning his head to gaze at the flickering fire. He had a handsome face. Cupped in the glow of the flames, even the lines on his forehead and around his eyes added to his rugged beauty.

"Unless?"

His eyes turned to me, glowed gold.

"Unless I find a mate. A woman with special powers, gifted by the goddess, who can cure my tainted soul."

I gulped, shrinking a little in his shadow. "How can you find such a woman?"

The corners of his lips quirked. "I already have."

KNUT

The woman shook like a leaf on the breeze. Her drying hair was soft as corn silk, her eyes wide and fawn colored. Her pulse fluttered in her throat and my hand itched to cover it.

I needed to remember to be gentle, to put her at ease. I was used to barking commands and leading men, not saying sweet things to a woman.

I sat, keeping distance between us, so as not to tempt the beast. My lungs filled with her lovely scent. My ears picked up the rapid patter of her heart.

"Tell me of your home at the abbey. Your childhood." I softened my tone. "I wish to know everything about my mate. One day, we will be able to share thoughts, and you will show me your memories."

Her eyes widened.

"That is the work of the mating bond. It will manifest between us naturally."

Hazel wet her lips. Nervousness tinged her scent. No doubt she was afraid of being joined to a warrior suffering under a curse, one she had just met.

The more I thought about it, the more the beast inside me raged to take her, claim her. Make her my own. I would bind her to me with an unbreakable bond, a link between our very souls.

I shifted closer and ran my hand down the fall of her hair. With a small sigh, she leaned into my touch. The fear in her scent eased and the beast backed down. "For now, you will tell me about your life."

The press of her lips told me she wanted to be stubborn and resist, but she obeyed.

"I lived all my life in an orphanage attached to an abbey. The nuns take in orphans from the surrounding villages— but only girls. I have many friends—closer than sisters. There are a few my age: Sage and Sorrel, Willow, Fern, Angelica and Rosalind. They will be worried that I disappeared." She gnawed her lips again. "I wonder what the friar will tell them."

"The friar is the one who sold you?"

"Yes. He oversees the grounds and all of us. The nuns keep us busy with gardening and weaving. The friar sells our cloth, herbs and honey, and sets the money for our dowry, so he can find us good husbands. At least, that's what he told us." She frowned, a line appearing on her otherwise smooth forehead. "One of my friends disappeared overnight. Sari was going to run away with her lover, but," Hazel shook her head, "Later in the village, I saw the lad mourning her. Sari never got free of the abbey. The friar found out she was leaving and gave her to the Corpse King."

"How do you know?"

Hazel looked away. "I saw her body in the cave. It was shrunken and dried, like an old husk. But it was her. Oh, Sari," She pressed her fist to her mouth as if trying to hold back her tears. They came anyway and I could hold back from touching her no longer.

I wrapped my arms around her, holding her shaking body as she wept.

"Hush, sweet one."

"It's my fault," she wailed. "I knew the friar was taking the money and hoarding it for himself. I saw him counting it one day and the greed on his face. Other girls had disappeared before. The friar told us they went to good husbands. But we never saw them again, even when they promised they would visit. I suspected, but I did not warn the others. Not until it was too late. The friar caught me, locked me in the room with Fleur, and then gave us to the Grey Men. They took us to the Corpse King's cave and that is where you found me."

"How did you escape the cave?"

"Fleur—she has powers. She somehow called the witch's staff to her."

"The one you now possess?"

"Yes," she reached for it, and I allowed her to grasp it and set it between us. "The friar broke it over his knee, but it magically appeared at our time of need."

"Fleur was rescued holding a piece," I told her what I'd learned from the pack bonds, before the storm and distance disrupted them. "She nearly killed the Corpse King with it. He lives," I cautioned as hope dawned on her face, "but he is weakened. You were meant to be his bride."

"What is he?"

"An ancient evil, a king who committed acts of atrocity I dare not speak of." I gathered her close, gratified when she pressed against me. Her body responded to me, even if she was still deciding if I could be trusted. "The mage is everything unnatural and his servants belong amongst the dead."

"Necromancy?"

I nodded. "It takes great sacrifice to sustain such awful power. Human sacrifice."

"He killed Sari. Who knows how many of my abbey sisters also died to feed him."

I did not tell her what my warriors had reported: a pile of bones stacked outside the cave.

Instead I cupped her chin. "Do not think of it, Hazel. You escaped and when we return to the mountain, we will find a way to protect all of your sisters."

"Thank you," and her small smile lit my heart like sunlight breaking through the grim day.

HAZEL

K nut's large hand palmed my head, dropped to my nape and gave it a squeeze. My body had relaxed in the warmth of his regard and the fire, but now my heartbeat picked up. His thumb stroked over the sensitive skin of my neck and tingles spread through my body, focusing on the points of my nipples and the valley between my thighs.

His eyes, which had dimmed as I'd shared my tale, flared brighter. He took his hand away.

"If I tell you to stay here, will you obey?"

"Yes."

"Good. You will not like the consequences if you don't." He reminded me of the punishment he'd dealt earlier, and the one he'd promised. Fire leaped into my blood at his stern look.

As soon as he shut the door, I rose and went to the window, wanting to see what form he would take next. A large silver wolf ran across the yard, tail brushing over dead stalks in the ill-tended garden as it trotted away.

I busied myself exploring the hut. I found a broom in the

corner, and poked at the cobwebs, cleaning up. A dank back room held mostly molded blankets, but to my delight, I found a pair of shoes and an overdress, folded in a chest of cedar. They were finely stitched—part of a bride's dowry.

I took them, saying a prayer for the missing people who'd left their valuables behind.

While I waited for Knut, I stripped off my shift and washed it as best I could in the bucket, setting it near the fire to dry. After adding a sprig of dried lavender to the water I'd set aside, I washed myself. My body, strong from hours of abbey chores, had changed with my recent adventure. My limbs and stomach had hardened, toned from running and little food, but my breasts were larger, almost swollen, as were the folds between my legs. I touched them carefully. Once a month, around the full moon, I suffered intense heat, a fever that left me gasping with need. Was it possible that my body was responding to the warrior?

I poked at my shift, willing it to dry faster so I could cover my traitorous body. Never mind that the fabric was so thin, it barely hid my responses. Never mind that he seemed to be able to scent my arousal and speak into my very thoughts.

I wanted to ask him why I heard his voice in my head, but didn't want him to think me mad.

A thump at the door had me whirling. A shriek died on my lips as the large wolf trotted in, a dead pheasant in its jaws. It stopped dead at the sight of me. It huffed, laid down the game, and trotted back out. The door swung shut.

I threw on my shift, ignoring the damp patches. Of course, the Berserker was going to return and see me. Shame burned in my cheeks as I realized a part of me wanted him to.

Once dressed, I hastened to the door and opened it to find Knut standing on the stoop.

It was my turn to stare. The warrior's broad, muscled form was bare except for a scrap of leather loincloth slung around his hips.

He faced west, watching the sunset. The storm had died, but the clouds remained, so the sinking sun was only a few red lines in a grey sky.

When he turned, he had a large white pelt in his hands. Something in me quivered as he approached and silently set the fur on my shoulders, tucking it snug around me.

My senses blazed to life. I smelled the lavender from my bath, the heavy rain waiting in the clouds, the earthy pine scent that clung to the pelt.

His large thumb brushed my cheek, dusting away a tiny flower that'd clung to my cheek. Drawing in a deep breath, he let his forehead sink to mine as his hand settled on my nape.

"Can you cook the pheasant?"

"Yes," I breathed.

His fingers flexed, squeezing the fragile bone, holding me still as his mouth touched mine. Desire flared in me, unfurling, a weight and a lightness both at my core.

I gasped and retreated. His eyes burned bright, but he let me go. I stepped back into the hut, and closed the door in his face, leaning against it for support. My hand trembled as I checked my breasts, my midriff, the tops of my thighs. I wasn't naked but I'd been stripped bare by that golden gaze. Even now heat pooled in my secret places, making me press my legs together against the ache.

What was happening to me?

"Hazel," Knut called after a moment.

Checking my flushed cheeks one last time, I let the door creak open between us.

Knut had pulled on his breeches and boots. I'd found a man's shirt among the crofter's things, but now I didn't want to tell him. The expanse of his muscled chest left me breathless.

"I'm sorry. I don't know what happened," my voice shook.

The corners of his eyes crinkled. "No matter." He had to stoop under the door frame. I backed away to make room, but it didn't help. His massive form dominated the space. He took one look at the freshly swept and cobweb free space, and smiled.

I couldn't help warming at the sign of his pleasure.

He passed me to pick up the pheasant. I shook myself and went to focus on my duty.

When the meat was roasted, Knut and I sat at the table together. The warrior gave me the larger portion and ate only with his left hand. His right found mine and held it under the table, the entire meal. I shifted once to strip tender meat off the bone and he let me go. As soon as I was done, though, he claimed my hand, first sucking the grease from my fingers and then resting both ours on his leg, his own fingers clamped around my wrist.

I didn't know what to say, so I said nothing. As he finished his meal, his thumb played over the sensitive skin. Wet heat kindled between my legs and I started shifting to ease the tingles. Knut didn't take his eyes off me, but I kept mine on my meal while my cheeks burned and burned.

"Finished?" he asked when my plate was a pile of bones.

I nodded. Frowned at the few scraps on his plate. "Did you eat enough?"

"The wolf had a few before he caught the fattest bird for you. Are you full?"

"Yes."

"Warm and comfortable?"

"Yes, thank you, sir."

His smile widened. "It does me good to hear it. Now," he tugged me to stand between his knees. "I told you there would be a reckoning."

"What?"

"Punishment, for your behavior in the ravine." He cocked his head to the side. "Were you ever punished at the abbey?"

"Yes. The nuns with switches. The friar threatened us with a paddle, but mostly locked us in the scullery or had us kneel on pebbles."

I drew up my skirt and showed him the little white scars.

Anger flickered in his face. "I will never mark you in this way. Not for punishment. You will wear my marks one day, but they will be marks of love." His large hand settled on my shoulder, lightly collaring half my neck. His thumb stroked over my pulse.

"I don't understand."

"You will, little one. Now," his tone turned stern. "You broke your word. You said you would obey and you did not. In the ravine, with the Grey Men, you ignored a direct order."

"They were going to kill you."

"I told you to run."

"I could not watch you die." I stared at the table until he caught my chin, drew my gaze to his.

"It is my right to protect and fight for you. Hazel, you could've been killed."

I worried my lip.

"You promised me."

"I know."

He straightened, pushed his chair back from the table. "Come here," he patted his lap.

I hesitated.

"Hazel, if you do not obey now, the punishment will be twice as long and hard." He held out a hand, I took it and let him pull me over his knees. In that moment, I could no more resist him than I could tell my own heart not to beat.

He slid my shift up, exposing me. His leg moved, tipping my bottom up higher. He would be able to see everything—my bare, quivering bottom, the down covering my flushed sex, my pale thighs underneath.

"Have you ever been punished in this way?"

"No, sir." It felt right to keep calling him that.

He chuckled. "Good girl." He cupped my left bottom cheek and set the place between my legs throbbing. I shifted and the thick rod of his cock grew under my belly.

His hand squeezed, hard. "Be still, little one." His voice was low and thick, guttural. "You do not want to tempt me anymore than you already have."

I craned my head and met his blazing golden gaze. Knut still held me but now the man was gone, replaced by pure predator.

His fingers slid into the crevice of my bottom and I whimpered. Not because it hurt, but because my sex leaked more cream, threatening to dampen his leg.

Knut went very still.

"You like this," he rasped. "You're ready for me, ready for —" Instead of finishing his thought, he slid his fingers lower. A few inches and he'd reach my aching core. I wanted to fight it, even as I wanted more.

He took his hand away, placing it on my back, as a whine escaped me.

"Hazel, I'm going to punish you now."

"Will it...will it hurt?"

"Yes," he said gently. "It must, to teach you. In the pack, orders must be obeyed immediately. I am a leader, at the top of the pack, but even I must obey my Alpha. Your punishment will be hard enough to chastise, but it will not truly harm you."

"I don't understand."

"You will."

His hand smacked down.

"Did that hurt, little one?"

I let out a breath I'd been holding.

"Yes, but not much."

He followed it up with another swat and I lost my breath again. When I struggled to get up, he held me fast and delivered a few more in rapid succession.

"Because you are new to this, I will only warm your arse. Next time you will heed me immediately or you'll receive double the discipline. Once over my knee and again with a leather strap leaning over a table or a log. You'll stand in the corner with your hands on your head in between."

My sex clenched.

His hand clapped down, I kicked, and he spanked my right bottom cheek and then the left, swatting playfully but with enough force to leave a sting. He wasn't using his full strength, not even close.

The pain pulsed in my secret places, making them even more slick. My wriggling squashed my breasts against his hard thighs and my nipples chafed against the unyielding muscle. I had to get away before the warm tendrils curling through me turned into an overwhelming blaze.

Knut struck again and I cried out as the heat turned into an inferno. My sex dripped.

"No," I tried to wrench myself away. "You must stop."

He caught my hands at my back and held them there. "Be still," he warned again. "You will be still and take your punishment."

His hand came down again, but this time massaging the sore flesh, soothing the ache. All the hurt spiraled away, leaving an intense throbbing, almost pleasurable.

"Oh, no," I whimpered."

"Trust me."

My bottom throbbed, sting penetrated the very core of me. My sex ached, longing for his touch.

"This is how wolves discipline their naughty mates," he told me. "Will you be good from now on and listen to me?"

"Yes," my voice came in a breathless rush.

His palm caught the underside of my bottom and I squeaked. "Yes, what do you call me?"

"Yes, sir."

"Good girl."

He busied himself laying down a volley of swats, covering every inch of my bottom. I danced on my toes, whimpering. It was just on the edge of what I could take.

I stopped trying to fight it and surrendered.

I lay limp over his legs by the time he stopped.

"And now punishment for hesitating to come to me just now," he said. "You will learn to obey immediately and run into my arms or to lie over my lap when I give the order. Open your legs, Hazel."

Slowly I widened my stance, head hanging down and hand clutching his leg, I closed my eyes for what I knew was to come.

First though, he only cupped my sex. He paused to

squeeze my bottom and his fingers slipped lower to handle my slippery folds.

"Ooooh."

He swatted once, twice, light slaps that didn't sting but reverberated through me in a different way. I gasped as heat rushed through me.

"Just a few more," he murmured.

A pause and then a heavy impact on my center. The force of it rocked me forward, but I pushed back again, eager for more. The tissues between my legs were lighting up, tingling, and coming to life with each smack. He swatted me again and again, until I gasped and bucked. The coil tightened inside me snapped, pleasure flooding my body.

"There you are," he said, stroking my back.

When I pushed up, he helped me to my feet and straightened my shift.

"You all right?"

I nodded. He cupped my cheek and I couldn't keep from leaning into his touch.

"So sweet," he murmured. "Such a fighter, but your body knows to whom it belongs."

I jerked back. I hadn't fought him at all. I was supposed to be stronger than this. To set my own course, go my own way. Not trust so freely or bend to a man's rule. Had I learned nothing from my time in the abbey?

Knut let me go. His cock pressed against the front of his breeches when he rose, but he ignored it.

"I'm getting more firewood."

As soon as he left, I felt his loss. I almost followed him. Instead, I moved to the window overlooking the garden.

The moon had risen. It would be full soon. That would bring a whole other host of trouble.

I kept my back stiff as he entered and tended the hearth.

The feelings Knut sparked during my spanking swirled through me. I barely knew this warrior and my body already responded to his touch. I'd never felt such pleasure. Already I craved more. I was warm, fed, and safer than I'd ever been. I'd all but forgotten my plans to escape. Instead of the warrior, my own desires kept me here.

"Hazel, come."

There was nowhere to run, but my feet dragged as I went to him. Immediately he took me onto his lap, on the blanket in front of the fire.

"Sweet little one." His thumb rubbed my cheek. "I know this is new and hard, but we will make it through. And you will learn the ways of being my mate."

Despite myself, I sighed and melted into him.

"I know I am rough with you. All my life I've been at war," he murmured in my ear. "When we are back at the mountain that is my home, you will meet the other females who've become Berserker brides. They will help explain what I cannot."

"Are all the pack women treated this way?"

"Yes, when they earn it. There are only four—all sisters. And now you. I do not know what I did to earn such a treasure, but I will spend my life in gratitude for it."

I squeezed my eyes shut. He knew his course. He was a warrior. It was so simple for him—he killed his enemies and took what he wanted. I was the one fighting battles within myself.

KNUT

I turned my woman to face me, only to find her eyes brimming with tears.

"Oh, little one." I was undone. I possessed no weapon to fight her sorrow. Her body responded to me as mine did to hers, but she was resisting her desires. I did not know why. I'd slay all her fears, if I could.

"You're so strong," I crooned. "I watched you face the Grey Men. Sweet and so brave, my lovely little mate."

Wrapping my arms, I drew her down on the bed I'd made before the fire.

After a few more shuddering sighs, she slept.

I nuzzled her neck, breathing in the scent of her hair.

My beast knew she was mine, I knew she was mine. Her body knew as well.

Her mind still had to decide.

I SLEPT LIGHTLY, and in the morning left Hazel curled in front of a cold hearth. The day was bright and fine, though storm clouds still swirled in the far away sky, right over the cave of the Corpse King. The mage was angry at the loss of his potential bride.

As I fetched water, found more firewood, and lay a few snares to catch our dinner, my head throbbed with a call coming over many leagues.

Berserkers under attack. Return home.

The many leagues between me and the mountain was enough to mute the pack bonds, but the Alpha bond was stronger. The old Knut would run through fire and death to obey the command. But now I had Hazel.

Return home.

My feet started west, the direction of the mountain. I found myself at the river before I could stop myself. When I did, my head pounded until I put up a shield in my mind.

I'd spent a lifetime obeying the Alpha's commands. But now I would resist them.

Letting Hazel sleep, I searched the grounds thoroughly, pleased when I found a root cellar with a few apples and potatoes still fresh in the cool space. If we stayed another night, I could hunt as a wolf and make sure she was well fed. As lovely as she was, I wouldn't mind plumping her up before the winter. The thought of curling up with her during the cold months, sating myself with her curves had my cock pressing against my breeches. My teeth gritted against the ache.

Detouring into the forest, I leaned against a tree trunk and freed my raging cock. A few minutes recalling Hazel's plump bottom upended over my knee and I spurted so hard I almost fell to my knees. Gasping, I sagged against the trunk, and fought for control. My vision flickered as the beast howled, trying to break free.

The Alphas on one side, the Corpse King on the other.

And the beast within, testing my fragile control. But I must risk it all to claim my mate.

I would defy the Alpha's command. I would not return to the mountain until she bore my mark and accepted my bond.

THERE WAS a cold scent on the breeze as I returned to the farm, carrying a new staff I'd cut from a tree and shaved clean. The clouds were drifting closer, the Corpse King searching for what he had lost.

I stilled as Hazel appeared, pink-cheeked and lovely, rubbing sleep from her eyes. My cock came to life all over again.

"Come," I rose and held out my hand. Pleasure curled through me as she obeyed.

After making sure there were no splinters left, I gave her the staff.

"What is this?"

"I am going to teach you to spar," I told her.

"Here? Now?" She glanced at the coming storm.

"To pass the time. We stay here until tomorrow. Tonight, you will eat well and rest again. This morning you will learn to fight."

She gnawed at her lip, holding the rod uncertainly.

"Shouldn't I just use the witch's staff?"

"That sort of power is best used sparingly. If it belongs to the witch I know, she will one day want it back." Truth was, I didn't even want my woman handling the scary stick. Magic always had a price.

"If you are quick enough, you may learn to best me," I told her.

She scoffed, but brightened a little, excitement creeping into her scent. She was so lovely, her limbs smooth and sturdy, her bare neck and shoulder calling for my mark.

A flush rose in her cheeks at my scrutiny and I grinned broader.

"Come, Hazel." I motioned to a spot in front of me. "Unless you are afraid?"

HAZEL

I frowned as I weighed the staff on my palms. Insufferable warrior. He stood bare-chested in leather breeches, perfect lips curved and mocking. A breathtaking array. My body had tingled as I woke surrounded by his scent. I'd lain there awhile, dreaming of the ghost of his hand playing over my eager flesh. The memory of him spanking me was enough to make me long to touch between my legs.

A tilt of his head told me he scented my arousal. Jerking up my chin, I resolved to hit him with the staff as much as I could.

I marched to face him.

"First we work on stance." He instructed me to stand with legs apart, planted firmly but lightly on the balls of my feet, ready for me to rock back or leap forward. He moved around me, positioning my arms and shoulders.

His touch had my body heating from more than the morning sun.

"The Grey Men are strong but do not anticipate the blows. You can rush them. Aim for their legs, do not try to overpower them. Use your speed. Your slight size. Duck and weave. Use your wits more than your brawn, and you can confuse them enough to have a chance to get away."

"You know this just from fighting them a few times?"

"Aye. Lives are lost in the seconds it takes to learn your opponent, long before he strikes the killing blow." He had me thrust and parry until my arms ached. As the sun rose high, he fetched the water bucket, and made me stop to eat some apples and dried meat, insisting when I refused.

"You are a good teacher," I told him between chewing.

"I was called upon to teach the young warriors."

"It is more than that," I guessed. "You are a good fighter. One of the best in the pack."

He inclined his head, a gracious movement followed by a sudden grin. "I will teach our sons to fight."

My brows lifted.

With swift steps, he closed the distance between us. As he bent down, his hand settled on the back of my neck, a possessive touch I liked far too much.

"Soon, I will mark you properly, so the pack knows you are mine. We will return to the mountain and celebrate our union for a whole moon. You will spend your nights on your back beneath me and your days in my arms, too sore to walk. Within the year, you will give birth to our first child."

My mouth dropped open.

"Tell me you don't want this," he challenged, raising his chin.

I could not answer. My cheeks heated and my body shook with desire. Fluid trickled between my lower lips. I was hot and ready for him.

But I shook my head. "Am I to have no choice?"

"You do not want one. Your body has chosen me," he

said smugly. His gaze dropping to my nipples, which were pointing through the dress I wore.

I put my hands on my hips.

"You said that many in pack need mates. Maybe when you bring me to the mountain, I will meet them all and then decide--"

My head snapped back as his hand fisted in my hair. "You are mine," he growled.

His eyes flared with gold light and I froze, pulse leaping in my throat, I stared down the predator in them. His fingers tightened in my hair, all gentleness gone. "If you run, I will chase you. If you resist, I will overpower you. Push me and I will take you to bed and spank and stimulate you over and over until you are hoarse from screaming my name."

His mouth slammed on mine. He turned me to him and held me fast, lips ravaging mine over and over. My knees buckled as heat blazed between our bodies, bringing every nerve ending to life. His fingers delved under the hem of my short dress and thrust into my wet sex. I arched up, my cries swallowed by his ruthless mouth.

My body went limp in his arms; I barely knew when he took his mouth away. He dragged me up against his hard chest, locking me against him.

"Do not tempt me, Hazel. I will use all my power to make you admit you are mine."

KNUT

L ate in the day, I washed my face in the stream. My head still throbbed with the pressure of resisting the Alpha's call. I was running out of time.

All afternoon Hazel had been quiet. I hadn't meant to scare her, but my control was so thin. It was all I could do not to pounce, drive her to the ground, and bury myself deep inside her. I'd fuck her hard and long, until she forgot everything but the feeling that we were one.

She deserved a stronger mate. I was stronger than most living things on earth, but I was not strong enough to let her go.

I dashed my reflection, marring the image before I headed back to the hut.

The storm had died away but the day was still cold, an unseasonal chill for the middle of summer. The smell of smoke on the wind made me uneasy. The Grey Men would not be able to cross the river, but the Corpse King might have other weapons.

Soon we'd have to return to the safety of the mountain. It was reckless to stay away from the pack, and dangerous.

The pack bonds helped control the beast. But I could not face my warrior brothers until I'd fully claimed my mate.

I'd always been respected in the pack, strong enough to stand alone when others succumbed to the Berserker rage. Berserkers like Leif and Brokk formed brother bonds between them, to aid each other's control. They'd share everything, even a mate.

I had never bonded with another warrior. I had no need of help--and I was glad of it, for I would not tolerate another man touching Hazel. But a lone wolf is a dead wolf. Too long alone, and the beast would claim my mind forever. Keeping away from the pack, resisting the Alpha's call, I risked both Hazel's life, and mine.

I had to find a way to woo this woman. I had to convince her she was mine, before it was too late.

I strode back to the hut. The girl was in the root cellar, choosing what vegetables to eat.

"Hazel," I bellowed. "Come inside."

She trotted over, potatoes gathered in her arms. My heart and cock leaped as they had the moment I first saw her. She looked at home here, hair in a thick braid, smooth, tan skin speaking of many hours working under the sun.

Arousal blazed in her scent as she grew closer to me. Her heartbeat thumped as loudly as mine.

She responded to me so well. Which made holding onto my control pure torture.

Her cheeks were bright red as she stopped on the doorstep.

"I am leaving to hunt," I told her. "You will stay in the house."

She nodded, unwilling to cross me after our last battle. I'd won her compliance with a kiss, but I'd not won the war.

I moved out of the way so she could enter the hut. She kept her eyes down until I caught her chin and forced it up.

"If there is danger, I will return quickly. You will heed my commands."

"Yes, sir."

"Good."

I ducked close to fill my lungs with her delicious scent. My cock fought to get out of my breeches and I let out a growl. *Go inside.* I sent the thought into her mind, testing the new bond between us. She must have heard it because she scuttled into the hut and slammed the door.

I waited a moment, fighting the beast. It would be so easy to tear the door off its pegs and ravage her.

My hand slammed the side of the hut, making it shudder. The beast within me prowled, scenting my weakness. How many hours, how many days before it broke free?

Forcing myself away, I stripped and Changed into the wolf. I'd hunt until dark and return with a brace of prey. Nothing said 'I will be a good mate' like a gift of dead rabbits.

Life was simpler as a wolf.

A FEW HOURS LATER, pleased with the results of my hunt, I followed a pleasant scent home. The woman must have put some herbs on the fire, for the smoke smelled sweet.

I took the time to wash in the stream and prepare the game I'd caught. The hunt had been long and successful. For now, the beast was quiet.

A large summer moon lit my path as I came through the garden to the hut. I stopped to add a few sprigs of a herb that would go well with the rabbits. The Change from wolf to man left me with another large, white pelt slung about my shoulders. Another gift for Hazel. The wolf liked her waking surrounded by its scent.

She met me at the door, cheeks flushed, almost glowing in the moonlight. I would've dropped to my knees and worshiped her as a goddess, if I hadn't been holding the rabbits.

"Knut," she gasped. Under the floral smoke, fear tinged her scent.

My instincts hummed to life. "What's wrong? Where is the danger?"

"No danger," she shook her head, but she was trembling. I went to gather her in my arms, chastise her for not keeping warm, and she jerked back. "Don't touch me."

"What is this? Are you all right?"

"It's nothing. Just my...sickness. It comes and goes with the moon," she clasped her hands in front of her, gave me pleading look. "You have to take me back to the abbey."

HAZEL

Frowning, Knut pushed me inside. He set what he was carrying on the table—a gruesome bundle of headless game.

When he faced me again, I noted that he was between me and the door. It did not matter; I could not fight him or escape, but I had to make him see.

The fever had started as soon as the moon rose. It came over me every full moon, but something—maybe the time spent in the warrior's embrace—brought it on early.

Knut loomed over me. "Tell me about this sickness."

"It is a curse, much like yours. It comes over us...a few of my abbey sisters and I." I wrung my hands. Just the sight of him made my mouth water, my sex dampen, my insides tighten with longing.

"How long does it last?"

"A few days. When I was at the abbey, the friar would lock up the women who went into heat. I would fall asleep hearing them moan and shriek like a demon possessed them."

"Did he lock you up?"

I shook my head. "I hid it from him. But it's worse tonight, so much worse. I ache. I almost...touched between my legs."

He paused. "You wanted to touch yourself?"

"Yes."

"But did not?" His voice was deeper, thicker.

I shook my head.

"Why not?"

"What?"

"Why did you not touch yourself?"

"Because it is wicked," I whispered. "It is the curse of the moon. I must not give in. You must help me." Every second that ticked by brought me closer to losing control, breaking down and wanting to rut against him like a dog in heat. Shame burned my cheeks. "Please help me."

"I will help you."

"You will take me back?"

Bright yellow light flared in his eyes. "No, Hazel. I will never let you go."

"Then what—"

He laid a finger over my lips. "Hush. I am your mate, and will give you what you need. You will trust me."

"I do not want to lose control."

"Then give yourself to me. I will keep you from harm."

I clutched at his forearms. "You must bind me. I will moan and beg, but you must not let me go. Please."

"All right," he said, his voice gruff.

He tied me to a sturdy chair using strips of soft leather he'd found.

"A rope will hold better," I told him.

"Nay, little one. I will not allow anything to chafe your soft skin." His touched brushed fire through me.

Almost in the throes of the sickness, I did not argue.

I relaxed only when I was fully bound. He'd set me close to the fire, in a stream of shining moonlight.

"You are very beautiful," he told me. His fingers brushed my lips, and I sighed, almost crying with relief. He could touch me and I could respond without fear of disgracing myself.

"Thank you."

He gave me an odd look and busied himself spitting and roasting the game. When it was done, he came with a bowl of meat and a knife. "You will eat," he ordered, slicing off bits to place into my mouth.

As he leaned over me, goosebumps rose on my naked flesh.

"Cold, little one?"

"No." Under the thin shift, my chest was flushed. Sweat trickled between my breasts. "It's nothing." I forced a smile.

Knut didn't look happy, but he kept to his task of feeding me.

I licked my lips, tasting the grease. He held another piece to my mouth and my tongue flicked out to taste it, and him.

Glancing at the moon, I flexed my legs in the bonds, but they held.

He rose to get more meat, the bulge in his pants at eye level. An aching wave of longing washed through me, pressure rising in my lower belly. My head fell back as I strained my hips upward.

Knut turned at my moan.

"What's wrong?"

"It's coming," I panted. "I don't..." I tossed my head back and forth.

"Hazel, tell me...what's going on?"

"So hot," I gasped. "Too hot."

"One moment," he grunted, and undid the bonds at my wrists.

"No—stop—"

With quick fingers, he lifted the gown over my head, whipping it off. Cool air washed over me. But now I was naked and half free.

"What are you doing?" I cried out even as my body leapt to life.

"I am going to help you." He knelt before me. "You will sate your lust with me. Submit to me, Hazel. I will break your heat and you will never suffer again." He put his hand on my thigh and it burned.

"No," I said. "I do not want this. I am not ready. Knut, please."

"You escaped the abbey, and those who kept you captive. Why do you not allow yourself to be free?"

I hung my head. "I...can't."

He moved away, and I began to struggle again. "Knut, don't leave me like this. You have to bind me, you have to help me—"

"Shh, shh little one. I am here. I will tie you again."

I sobbed in relief when my hands were secure.

"Hazel, do you trust me?" The big warrior had a bucket of water and a small pelt in his hand.

"What are you going to do?"

"Shhh. I will make you feel better." He dipped the fur in water and wrung it out before press its silky coolness against my hot skin.

"Better?"

"Yes," I sighed. He washed my body this way and I submitted to his touch. "It feels so good."

"More food?"

I nodded, but this time when his fingers touched my

lips, I sucked them inside, laving frantically until he pulled them away, groaning.

"None of that teasing, Hazel."

"Or what?" I purred.

"Or I will untie you and blister your bottom before putting you on your knees to serve my cock."

I gasped. My hips started rocking.

"Knut, please."

With a curse, he crouched in front of me. "What is it, little one? Tell me what you need."

My nipples crinkled as he passed his gaze over them.

"My breasts. They ache."

"Beg, Hazel. Beg me for what you want."

"Touch them, please." My mind was gone, all thought pushed out by the arousal pounding in my brain. "Please," I strained towards him. "I will die if you do not touch me."

"All right, all right, hush." His rough hands cupped my flesh and I sighed into his touch.

"Thank you. I need more. I need—"

He was already kneading them, brushing his thumb against my nipple in a way that sent pleasure shooting straight to my sex. I begged in wordless moans as he pinched my nipples, first lightly, then applying more and more pressure.

"Does that hurt?" He watched my face closely.

Arousal followed the sting, washing any pain away. "No. More."

He did as I asked, but I felt nothing but the overwhelming waves of desire, lapping against my sex.

Knut bent over me, frowning in concentration. His lips were so close to my skin...

My body arched up towards his, pushing until the bonds constricted my flesh.

"Calm yourself." He massaged me, pressing me back down.

My breath came in shallow pants. "I...can't..." Liquid dripped from me. Pooling on the chair, wetting my bottom and thighs. "I am so lost." Tears pricked my eyes. "Knut, I do not know why I am like this. I have tried to resist. I have prayed and prayed--"

"Shhhh," he soothed and bent his head, taking my nipple between his teeth.

"Oh," I cried out, hips dancing, jerking in invitation. "Oh, yes."

"You like that?" he gave me a little grin and the moon-light shone off his sharp front teeth. Without waiting for answer, he bowed his head and licked at my breast.

"Ahh," I let out a half moan, half sigh. Tears leaked from my eyes.

The giant warrior stayed kneeling before me, blond head bent to give me pleasure. His mouth worked its way down my bare body. Slowly, so slowly he tongued the crease between my legs and mound, lapping up my honey.

I held my breath, willing him to go closer, to touch the place I needed him most.

When he laid his mouth on my sex, the heat of his mouth matching mine, pleasure flooded through me. His tongue delved deep and I sobbed in happiness, rocking as much as I could in my bonds.

When he raised his head, still wet from my mound, I shuddered. My scent mingled with his, potent and right. We belonged together, our bodies entwined as closely as our flesh would allow. I wanted him on me, inside me. I wanted to be filled with his essence. I wanted him.

"Take me," I begged. "Knut, I am ready. I want to be yours." *I want to be one.*

His fingers skated over the tops of my thighs and I knew he'd heard my mental message. "Are you a virgin, little one?"

"Yes."

"You are ready for all of me?"

Freeing my hand, he pressed it to the front of his pants. I traced the thick bar of his cock, marveling at the size. "Yes."

Gently he pulled my hand away.

"I will pleasure you, but will not take you. You will learn my body, learn my voice. Lean into me like the flower turns to the sun. Then, and only then, will I mark you and make you mine."

I sobbed. "Please."

He entered me with rough fingers. My cunny clamped down on the digits, my inner muscles fluttering, working, desperate. Sweat poured down my body.

A low keening filled the air—cries of wanting torn from the deepest part of me.

Knut added lips and tongue to his fingers and I was undone. I screamed and fluid gushed over his hand. My climax claimed me over and over, as I writhed in my bonds.

He untied me and rubbed the red crisscrosses on my skin, before holding my exhausted body close.

Knut, I reached for him in my mind, a delicate joining, intimate, gentle.

I'm here. He clasped me tighter.

"You're all right, lass. You're with me."

"I can hear you," I gasped.

I know. "'Tis the bond."

I raised my head and touched his lips in wonder.

"This is the beginning," he said. "We are bound now by more than flesh and blood. You will not leave me."

KNUT

"I'd like to wash," Hazel told me. She didn't deny my words but kept her face averted from mine.

"What is wrong?"

"Nothing," she said and rose and went to the bucket. "I need to fetch water."

I met her at the door and blocked her way. "I'll get it."

"There's no need," she said stiffly. "I can do it."

"Are you angry with me little one?"

"No." She glared at the ground.

I'd give my life for this woman. I'd slay all her enemies. I wished they were here, now, so I could slay them, instead of wondering what else to say. "Something is wrong. You are crying."

"I'm not." She dashed at her eyes.

I growled. "I will spank you until you tell me."

She threw the bucket on the ground, narrowly missing my foot. Her temper only made me harder and I bit back a grin. My little rabbit was a fighter.

"I am ashamed," she said and wiped all my humor away.

"Why?"

"I am cursed."

"Hazel, it is no curse." I caught her hand before she could turn from me. "It is your gift."

"What?"

Her pained look wrung my heart. "Oh, little love, they lied to you. They told you lies to control your lust, to keep your true power in. But now you can let it out, you are safe with me."

"How am I safe? I will want things...." The tears pouring down her cheeks made me ready to hurt someone. "Things I should not want. I do not know how to keep them back. I am like a demon, a possessed woman."

"'Tis only your mating heat."

"It is lust. It is wrong."

"No, it is natural," Pulling her close, I cupped her sex. "Feel this. Feel how we are together." Automatically, she pressed against me, her hips working against my hand until the damp between her legs soaked my skin.

"No." she wrenched herself away. "I thought the fever was past, but it is not. You should tie me up again—"

"Why?" I gritted my teeth against my own arousal. "You are already bound. Your chains are in your mind."

"I'm getting water," she said. Grabbing the bucket and darting around me before I could stop her.

Shaking my head, I followed.

Her shift-clad form in the moonlight stirred my blood. By the time we reached the river, my cock was so hard I thought it might burst from my clothes. With great satisfaction, I shucked off my breeches.

"Give me that," I strode to her and snatched up the bucket. She turned, hissing, her mouth dropping open when she saw I was naked.

I went to the river and waded right in. The cold made

me yelp like a pup, but did nothing to ease my ardor. Cursing, I submerged myself and came up with a shout.

Hazel stood on the bank, a still, white figure. She could've been a specter, formed from moonlight to torment my dreams.

After flinging water off my hair, I stalked towards her, water streaming off my shoulders. My cock still jutted out from my body, hard and angry.

"You are not the only one who is cursed," I reminded her. "There is nothing you can do to hurt me. Except withhold yourself."

"My guardians at the abbey—"

"Were idiots. They did not understand who you are. They locked you away. But now you're free and you're still locked in a prison of your own making." I reached to touch her and stopped short, a finger hovering at her lips.

"You want this," I murmured, and watched as a tremor went through her. "So, Hazel, what's it to be?"

HAZEL

I t was all I could do to keep my eyes on Knut's face and not the hard organ ready to pierce me. I wet my lips and his gaze darkened.

"I am afraid."

"Then come to me. I will fuck you until there is not a thought in your head. For you are mine and you have nothing to fear."

I leaned towards him, so tempted. "I will not be controlled again, as I was in the abbey. I am not strong enough to survive that."

"You are stronger than you know." He sighed. "I will not let you go, Hazel, I cannot. It will mean my death. But this connection, this connection we have. It is more than feelings. We belong together, one soul in two bodies."

I shook my head.

"That thought frightens you?" he asked gently.

"I don't know why you care for me."

"Truly?" he snorted. "There is not one thing about you that doesn't make me want to possess you."

When I didn't answer, he shook his head. "I suppose you

want to know the reasons and will make me stand here, naked, while I list them all."

"You're the one who took off your breeches."

"Aye it was that or tear right through them." He sighed again and the movement made his sizable erection bob. "Very well. It was your scent that called to me from the first."

I waited.

"You know, most female wolves would be happy with a few dead rabbits."

I crossed my arms over my chest. "I am not a female wolf."

He cocked his head, studying me. "Take off your shift. If I am to bare all, then you must as well."

With trembling hands, I did as he bade. As always, his tone compelled me. As soon as the shift fell to my feet we both knew my true feelings, for I was wet, wet and ready.

"Hazel," he breathed.

"It's late," I interrupted. "We should return to the hut."

"Do not run from me." he growled.

In the moonlight, I could see every line and shadow on the planes of his face. Knut the man was almost gone and the beast had taken over.

"If you run, I will chase you. I will lay you down and take you in any way I please and will not stop until I've had my fill."

Despite myself I took a step back.

"Hazel," he warned.

I licked my lips, deciding.

Whirling, I ran.

For a moment, I thought I might reach the hut. My feet beat a frantic rhythm against the forest floor, breath raging in my throat. Just before I broke from the woods, strong arms clamped around me, lifting me even while my legs pumped the air.

"Be still," the words tore from a barely human throat. Knut dragged me back to the riverbank to where he'd flung his clothes. His hands when he laid me down on the garments were gentle, but when I struggled he held me down.

"Be still," he ordered and my spine unhinged at his guttural bark.

Satisfied at my stillness, he grasped my legs, pulled them open.

I quivered, chanting under my breath, "Yes, yes."

For all his intent chase, he took his time looking over me. My sex was wet and dripping as he bent, sniffed, and licked up the length of my thigh. When he nuzzled between my legs, I buried my hands in his hair. He nipped my lower lips. Grasping my wrists, he pinned them at my sides.

"Oh yes," I gasped again.

He set the broad head of his cock at my entrance. As wet as I was, his entry still burned.

"Do not fight me little one," he coached. "Breathe."

Slowly he pushed in, I stretched, gulping. He hit my barrier and I cried out in pain.

His hand closed over my breast, squeezing, sending a fresh wave of pleasure through me.

"Deep breath," he said and snapped his hips, tearing into me.

I cried out.

He cradled my head, raining kisses on my face. "Never again. It will never hurt again."

Already the pain was fading. I closed my eyes, savoring his satisfying weight on my small frame, his arms and legs caging me. I was safe forever, in his arms.

Look at me, his voice purred in my thoughts.

I did.

Our minds are one. Our bodies are one. You will heal quickly now.

Warmth curled through me, he moved a little and I felt him where our bodies joined, a perfect fit. My body had already adjusted to the brutal stretch.

I locked my legs around his hips.

"That's it, little one. Take me deep."

My hips undulated against his, gently at first, then with a more demanding speed. His thick cock speared me, pressing against every part of my womb, filling me to the brim with undeniable pleasure.

"Is this how it is?" I asked in wonder.

"This is how it is," he said. "But only with you. And for me there is no other."

My small arms pulled him closer. There was nothing evil here, in the circle of our bodies. It was the sweetest feeling and I'd die happily in this place.

I wouldn't, Knut growled in my mind. *I need at least a thousand years to enjoy your lovely flesh.*

I scratched my nails down his back and felt his muscles ripple against me. He moved faster, thrusting into me. His heavy balls slapped my center with delicious force.

"This first time, I'll be gentle."

"This is gentle?" I gasped.

He turned his head and nipped my ear. "I have waited so long."

"I know. Take your pleasure." I slid my arm around his shoulders, hanging on as his hips pounded into me. My orgasm rose rapidly, blowing up like a gale that bows all but the largest oak before it. I howled my delight and shuddered as Knut's cock pulsed once, twice, and released his seed deep inside me.

"Hazel," he said my name over and over, kissing me until I laughed.

He rolled to his back, bringing me with him so I sprawled over the giant shelf of his muscled chest. His organ was still inside me. "How was your first time?"

"Good," I told him shyly.

"Not too painful."

"No." The feeling of being torn had faded right away.

Knut pressed his face into the crook of my shoulder and neck. His large hand cradled my head; my fingers sifted through his hair.

"Knut?"

"Mmm?"

"Why do you say I am brave?"

He made to move and I held him tighter, keeping us cheek to cheek so I did not have to meet his eyes. He rubbed my back, soothing.

"I have fought many battles, and seen courageous acts. There is none to match when you stood at my side to fight the Grey Men, even though you trembled in fear."

"I didn't fight at the abbey. I didn't save Sari, or Fleur."

His fingers found the nape of my neck, squeezing reassuringly. "You couldn't save them, but you will save many others."

I rose up then, gazing down at him.

"When we are back at the mountain," his index finger traced my lips, "I will go to the Alphas and tell them of the Corpse King's evil plan. The women at the abbey will all be rescued, I swear it."

I held my breath. It was too overwhelming to think of all

my friends--Willow, Fern, Sage, Sorrel, Rosalind, Angelica--
by my side again. Safe.

"Who knows? Some may be fit to be Berserker brides,
like you."

"What if they don't want to be mated?"

"I'm sure their warriors will convince them." He grinned.
"I'm an old warrior, but I wooed you in a few days."

His finger teased my lips. I turned my head and caught it
between my teeth.

His chuckled rumbled through my body. "Such a fighter.
Little rabbit." He cupped my cheek and looked at me so long
and with such love, tears filled my eyes.

"Hazel, I told you I wanted you from the first time I
caught your scent. And again when I saw you. But when you
stood against the Grey Men with me and did not flee, I knew
I wanted you by my side forever."

"You spanked me for that."

"Yes," he showed his fangs. "and will again, to drive such
valor out of you. It will not do to have you fighting battles
when you are carrying our sons."

I pressed my lips together to keep from smiling at him.
"How do you know they will be sons?"

He rolled us over, our bodies still joined, his burly arms
and chest caging my body. My eyes widened as his cock
turned to steel.

"Because," he flexed his hips, and filled me further. "I
will not stop claiming your body until we have many sons,
and daughters too."

KNUT

Hazel moaned in my ear and I came awake with a start.

We lay on a bed of soft pine needles, my body curled around hers. The goddess only knew how often I had claimed her last night, but it had been enough to make us fall asleep on the ground.

Fog drifted over us. It should be dawn but the world was grey.

"It's all wrong," Hazel muttered and thrashed in the throes of a bad dream.

"Little one." I shook her awake.

"Knut? Where are we?" She was cold, her face pale as last night's moon.

"In the forest, where I made you fully mine."

The wind whistled through the trees, but did not dispel the fog. The thick cloudy air advanced like an army of ghosts.

Hazel shivered and I tucked the pelt around her.

"Come. We need to get you close to the fire." I drew her up, keeping her close as I pulled on my clothes. Her shift lay a few feet away and I kept hold of her as I went to fetch it.

"Is it morning?" she asked.

"Yes. But the fog has stolen it away."

I turned to the direction I knew the hut lay in and faced a wall of fog, too thick to see through.

"Come," I said, forcing confidence into my tone. "This way."

But as we walked and walked, we reached nothing.

"Cold," Hazel muttered. A few feet later, she sighed.

"Are you all right, little one?"

"My head hurts."

"Your head and my cock. You wore me out," I said when she gave me a look.

The humor lasted only a few more steps. Something moved in the fog and I growled, fear like acid in my gut. I was an idiot to not see this for an attack.

"Back to the river." I pushed her along, ahead of another thick billow of fog. The air thinned somewhat when we reached the water.

"Knut, what is it?" Hazel's teeth chattered. I swung her up in my arms and crossed the body of water. The fog was less here, but still rising.

"The Corpse King is coming after you. He is drawn to your heat, but I will protect you, above all."

We walked through the forest, fear eating my heart. I did not have my axe, but what weapon would stand against the weather? Better we lay down and wait it out, although then the Grey Men would find us and all would be lost.

No way out. No hope.

Deep down, my beast was raging, howling with violence as if the enemy were here and on the attack.

"The fog affects the mind," I said suddenly.

"Yes," Hazel said, sounding very tired.

My skin prickled as the wind picked up, pushing the fog our way.

"We must run." I pulled her along, only to race straight into another thick bank of fog.

Hazel stumbled and I lost hold of her.

"Knut," she cried, suddenly sounding far away.

"Hazel," I grabbed for her. My arms closed around her, but the storm swirled around us, a voice on the wind chanting with evil purpose. The Corpse King. No wonder my beast was fighting for control.

"Come face me like a man," I shouted. The chant turned mocking.

I reached out via the pack bonds, trying to call for help. I was a fool to isolate myself from my Berserker brothers. My distrust of them put my woman at risk.

A gust of wind struck my body. Cowering before it, I covered Hazel as best I could, but when I rose the fog was a cage, four thick walls around us. With a little murmur, Hazel slipped out of my arms.

"No," I reached for her, coming back with only armfuls of smoke. "Hazel!"

Silence.

Hazel. I reached out via our minds and found her thoughts full of despair.

Dark. Dirty. Unworthy.

"Hazel," I called, keeping my voice calm. "Where are you? Hear my voice and come to me."

"I can't, Knut." When she finally answered, her voice sounded small. "I am too weak. You should leave me."

I pushed towards her voice and it was like wading through water.

"The Corpse King is using lies to make you despair."

I am weak. I gave into lust. My desires are filthy, taint everything they touch.

I am in your mind, little one. You are not dirty or wrong.

Hazel fell silent under the screeching wind, the Corpse King laughing at me.

"I will not let you have her," I bellowed. Claws sprouted from my hand.

I waded forward and almost tripped over a small form. My woman, curled into a sad little ball.

"Little one," I had her in my arms, chafing her cold skin. "Oh, Hazel, why are you so afraid?"

"You should leave me," she choked on a sob. "Save yourself. They will not come after you, if they have me."

"No, never." I lifted her and strode until we reached a tree. I set her against the trunk, surrounded by the comforting scent of pine. "You are mine, and I will never let you go. I will not surrender to an army. They can no more take you from me than they can take my soul."

"They want my soul," she said in a terrified whisper. "They are coming for it."

"They cannot have it." Fisting my hand in her hair, I kissed her and she opened herself to me with a shuddering sigh, accepting the warmth that poured through her body from mine.

You are mine. Touch me, Hazel. Feel my need.

My tongue probed her as my cock strained against my breeches. Still claiming her mouth, I freed myself. One thrust and I was inside her blessed heat. Her muscles shuddered around me, pulling me in deeper, calling me home.

Feel this, little one. This is real.

"Knut," she breathed against my mouth.

"That's it. Say my name. Remember I am yours." *I pledge my life to you.*

Her legs closed around my hips and I hitched her up, driving deeper. Her head flew back against the tree trunk, her perfect lips parted.

"I love you," she mouthed and drove me to my knees.

Carefully, I laid her on her back, her hair spread over the ground.

Mark her, my beast commanded and I could resist no longer.

Sweeping her hair off her shoulder, I bent her head to the side. My fangs pierced her.

Power. Heat. Lightning whipped through our bodies. She came, convulsing around my cock. I plowed deep inside her, filling her with my seed and my thoughts—all the force of my love filling her mind, driving the Corpse King out.

"Knut," she said, in between returning my frantic kisses. "What is happening? What did you do?"

I brought her hand to the marks on her shoulder. They were already healing.

"We are joined forever, little one." You are in my mind, as I am in yours, and we will never be alone.

Around us, mist swirled.

She will never be yours, a dark voice whispered.

I raised my head as bleak despair poured into my mind.

Fur rippled down my arm. I cried out as my spine stretched and snapped, my body contorting with magic. Pulling away from Hazel, I stretched out my hand and watched it turn into a massive claw.

"No—" I staggered back. "Hazel...run." I gasped as my bones broke and reknitted. The Change was upon me, and it hurt like never before.

"Knut! What is happening?"

"The beast," I choked out. I had marked her too late.

The fog swirled around us, echoing with mocking laughter.

Your strength is useless, warrior. The Corpse King's voice sliced through my control. *How will you save her from me if you cannot even save her from yourself?*

"Go," the word turned into a howl as my jaw and throat reshaped itself. *Hazel, you must leave before it's too late.*

"No, Knut, stay with me." Hazel's small hands grasped my body. Already my vision was turning red.

Forgive me. I have failed you. My skin became fur, and I jerked away from her.

"You cannot leave me," she cried.

She was at my side, sobbing, pulling on my arm. I snarled, and she cringed back.

Do you see this? Do you see the monster I become? I will not let you shackle yourself to me.

"No." Even with fear in her scent, she rose up and faced me. "You rescued me. We belong together. You set me free."

I am a warrior only. Not fit to be a mate.

"Knut," she reached for me again and I roared. When she cowered, I stretched myself over her. The beast scented a frail, trembling woman. It wanted to possess her.

Tears streaming down her cheeks, she tipped her head back and offered her throat. *Take me then. I am yours.*

Surrounded by the stinking mist, I nuzzled her and buried my face in her hair. She smelled of Hazel, of heat and love and strawberries.

Her voice touched my mind. *It's the Corpse King, trying to control you. Do not listen to him. Stay with me.*

I whined. Her breath shuddered in her. She was afraid, but she remained still underneath my body. So small and innocent. Such a fragile pulse. So easy to destroy.

No. I reared back, baring my teeth at the unseen enemy.

My claws tore into my own flesh. I would rip out my own heart before I hurt her.

"Stop!" Hazel reached for my bloody hands, and I pushed her away.

A sound in the fog—the cadence of marching feet. I whirled.

It's too late for me, I told her. *I will die so you might be free.* With a final shout, I leapt to face her enemies.

HAZEL

Knut, I screamed, but he'd blocked my mind. I ached, sensing the emptiness where he'd once been. The connection had lasted only a few moments but I felt the loss of him like a severed limb.

I staggered to my feet, pressing forward in the thick mist. I had to find him.

In the distance, Knut bellowed.

A giant shape loomed out of the mist. A warrior with golden eyes. Then another, and another.

I stumbled backwards and hit a hard, armored body. The Berserkers were at my back and front, hemming me in.

"What's this?" A large hand tugged my hair. I slapped at it, and burly arms grabbed me, held me fast.

"A woman."

More hands on my legs. "She smells delicious."

"She's in heat." The voice was thick with lust. "A spaewife."

"Is she unclaimed?"

"No," I kicked hard, and my foot struck the warrior

holding my legs until he dropped me. "I am Knut's. You cannot have me!"

"Knut?" The warrior at my back set me down, turned me to face him. He was a large and blunt-faced brute, but his hands were gentle. "I did not know Knut had a woman."

"He does now. He is mine," I snarled as savagely as a Berserker in the grip of madness.

The Berserker blinked in surprise. A few others chuckled.

"Wait, stop!" Another warrior called out. A redhead pushed through the circle of warriors. "You are Hazel? This is the girl Knut went to rescue," he said when I nodded.

"Is this true, Leif?" Asked the brute holding me.

"It is true," Leif jerked his head at me. "She is why he defied the Alpha's commands."

"Then she comes with us." With a grunt, the warrior lifted me.

"Wait!" I fought, "Let me go!" *Knut!* I reached out and heard him roar in impotent rage. The warriors must have restrained him, to keep him from me, but when I reached by my mind, he was silent.

Panicked, I began to struggle harder.

"Put her down, Thorbjorn. She is Knut's," Leif said. "She smells of his seed."

Thorbjorn grunted again, but set me on my feet.

Hands shaking, I pushed my hair back and showed the mark at the tender junction of my neck and shoulder. The magic had done its work; the mark was red and shiny but already healing. I hoped it would never fade.

"He marked you?" Leif and the others crowded around, but did not touch me.

"I am his mate. Where is he?"

"He's in the hands of the warriors he tried to attack. He will answer to the Alphas for that, and his crimes."

"What?" I breathed. I tried to push out of the circle of warriors, but they might as well have been made of stone.

"Enough, lass," a stern-faced warrior blocked my path. "Let's get out of this fog, and to the mountain."

They formed a circle around me, four walls of weapons, shields and hard-muscled bodies. As we marched, I kept reaching out with my mind, needing the touch of Knut's thoughts on mine. But there was only silence.

The further we walked, the more my mind cleared. The fog slowly dissipated, but my head throbbed with the loss of the bond.

"Are you tired?" Leif asked me.

I shook my head. "How did you know my name?"

"Your story has been shared throughout the pack. Fleur returned to us, and told us how you fought to rescue her, and made your escape from the Corpse King's cave."

I nearly stumbled. "Fleur is here?"

"Yes. She is safe." Leif's hand hovered near me, ready to catch me if I fell, but he took care not to touch me.

"Will...will I be able to see her?"

"Her, and her mates. She thrives within their care."

"What about Knut?"

"The Alphas will decide," another warrior answered before Leif could. "He will go before the Alphas to answer for his sins."

"Brokk," Leif said in warning tone, and the other subsided, shaking his head.

"What sins?" I asked.

"The Alphas tried to reach out to Knut, but he shut them out and resisted their orders to return to the pack. It made him unstable, and allowed his beast to almost consume him."

"He did not lose control. He didn't hurt me, he held back." I choked on my words. He'd said we were mated, was my love not enough to lift the curse? "I was safe with him. He protected me."

"He dishonored himself, and the pack when he defected to claim you."

"Please, I must see him. You must let him speak to me." *Knut,* I searched for his mind. *Do not shut me out. Let me know you're all right.*

"He is under guard until he sees the Alphas. They will decide his fate."

"His fate?"

"If the Alphas find him guilty of losing control, he may be deemed too unstable to take a mate," Leif said. "He may choose the ultimate punishment to salvage his honor."

I gulped. "What punishment is that?"

Brokk's voice was grim. "Death."

THE SUN SHONE brighter as we neared the mountain, but my thoughts plunged back into despair. Even if the Alphas pardoned Knut, showing mercy because we'd been under the Corpse King's attack, Knut would not return to my side if he believed he was unworthy to be my mate.

Then what would become of me?

At the foot of the mountain, two women sat on stones, hands folded in their lap. They rose as we approached.

"Go to them." Brokk rumbled. Leif nodded encouragingly.

Aware of my ragged dress and wild hair, I picked up my

skirts and approached them. One dark-haired and one blonde. The closer I got, the more familiar they looked.

"Hazel?" the blonde called, and I halted. She and the second woman closed the distance.

"I am Sabine," the blonde told me. "This is my sister Muriel."

"Welcome," Muriel said in a voice I recognized somehow. "We have been expecting you."

"Do you know Fleur?" I blurted. "You look like her."

"She is my twin," Muriel smiled. "Sabine is our older sister."

"Come," Sabine said. "We heard all about your escape from the Corpse King and your journey with Knut. You must be ready for some refreshment."

"The Alphas will want to question her," Brokk said.

"Not until she has rested," Sabine's tone turned sharp. She took one of my arms, and Muriel took the other. Ignoring the rest of the warriors, the sisters led me away.

They brought me to a great lodge built into the side of the mountain. Two guards waited in front of the great doors.

"We need water and firewood," Sabine told them with all the haughtiness of a queen. After a glance, the two warriors nodded and trotted away.

"There," Sabine pushed the doors open. "Now we have some privacy."

Inside, the lodge was beautifully furnished with carven chairs, a table full of bowls of food. There was a bed at the back, piled high with furs. Bundles of herbs hung from the rafters, filling the place with a lovely scent. A fire already burned in the hearth, a few cauldrons full of water warming beside it.

"Do you like your new home?" Muriel asked. Sabine went immediately to the fire and picked up one of the cauldrons, emptying it into a stone bath before adding a handful of herbs.

I nodded, speechless.

Sabine motioned for me to strip and get in the bath.

Muriel sat on a bench, picking up a gown and needle and thread. "Fleur told us your size. We will get you new gowns when it is safe again to go to market. Until then, I will alter a few of ours."

"Come, Hazel," Sabine beckoned. "The water will grow cold."

I sat in the tub while the sisters bustled about, setting out food, sewing my new clothes, and helping me wash. They were gentle and kind, full of cheery banter and sisterly teasing. Just like my fellow orphans at the abbey.

But I could not relax.

"Where is Knut?" I asked when I was dry and dressed. "I wish to speak to him."

"He arrived ahead of you, and went straight to speak to the Alphas," Sabine sat behind me to comb out my wet hair.

"Is he in trouble."

"That depends." Muriel handed me a bowl of stew, but I was too nervous to eat.

"Hazel, did he hurt you in anyway?"

"No. Never. Not even when he turned into the beast. Please, you must tell the Alphas." I turned and grasped Sabine's hand.

Gently, she freed herself, and lifted my hair off my shoulder, studying my mark. I resisted the urge to cover it with my hand. It was evidence of an intimate act. I did not like it being on display.

"Fleur told us of her time at the abbey," Sabine said finally. "Hazel, do you experience the mating heat?"

"I--," my face flushed. "Yes."

"We believe you are a spaewife. A special race of women who can mate with the Berserkers."

"I know. Knut told me."

"There are very few of us and we are all precious to the pack. That is why Alphas do not allow unstable wolves to mate."

"PIease," I rose, wringing my hands. "Knut isn't unstable. He was fighting his rage. The fog—the Corpse King's magic affected his mind."

"The Alphas will be merciful," Muriel soothed.

"It is your bond that might save him," Sabine said. "Do you understand how the bonds work?"

I shook my head.

"I will explain, but you must eat." Sabine waited until I had settled down at the table and forced down a few bites. "There are several different types of bond. Every member of the pack is linked. The alphas have a strong bond with every wolf. Then there are brother bonds that form between two or three wolves."

"Brother bonds?" I asked.

"It usually happens when two wolves save each other's lives. The brother bonds link two warriors closer than any other in the pack. It aids them in resisting the curse."

"Does Knut have such a bond?"

"No. He is an exceptionally strong warrior. Almost a lone wolf. But the beast almost claimed him in the end," Sabine mused.

Muriel cleared her throat. "The brother bond allows two men to share a mate."

"Share?" My mouth fell open.

"Yes," Muriel's cheeks were bright pink. "I am mated to two wolves."

"As am I," Sabine said, amused. "Fleur's mated to three."

"Three?" I shook my head. One giant warrior claiming me was enough. I could not imagine two. Or three.

"There is one bond that is stronger than all the rest," Sabine continued. "The mating bond."

Muriel was nodding her head.

"There are signs of a Berserker's true mate. A mating heat," Sabine raised a finger to indicate each, "A mating bite, which heals quickly as the Berserker shares his magic. And a mating bond that links the mind."

"We are able to hear our mate's thoughts," Muriel explained.

"Knut and I are linked." I looked down. He was still blocking me.

"When did you first hear him in your mind?"

"From the first. I saw him in the woods, and he came to rescue me from the Grey Men. That was when I first heard him."

Muriel and Sabine exchanged glances. "That is the earliest I've heard a mating bond form," Sabine said. "Perhaps the magic around the Corpse King's cave helped."

"Or perhaps Hazel was ready." Muriel touched my arm.

I set down my bowl and tucked my feet up on the bench, wrapping my arms around my legs. "I do not know what to think of all this."

The sisters watched me chew my lip.

"What is it like with Knut?" Sabine asked.

I blushed.

"I think that's all the answer we need," Muriel murmured.

I had a horrible thought. "Knut told me I could lift the curse, but then his beast took over anyway. Perhaps I am not his true mate after all..."

"That is not how the mating works," Sabine said with a

sigh. "The beast still lives inside them. It still hungers for dominance, but your presence sates its great need. When the desires claim Knut, you will be able to satisfy him."

"But...then what about my heat?"

"You will still go into heat. It is...uh...different." Even Sabine blushed. "More intense. But pleasurable, when you have mates by your side."

"Are there others at the abbey who go into heat?" Muriel asked.

"Yes. All of them," I frowned. "Except the youngest. We all are cursed."

"'Tis not a curse, Hazel," Sabine said gently. "'Tis your power."

"That is not what I was taught."

"And now you are mated to a fine warrior. He will teach you anew."

And gladly punish me until I learned. The thought made my cheeks heat, and heart race. I shook my head.

"I know I cannot go back to the abbey. I must face this new life. It is just so different, and strange."

"It is," Muriel said in her gentle voice. "Give it time. You will thrive here."

"Spaewives were meant to mate with Berserkers," Sabine added.

"I do not know if I will make a good mate."

Muriel looked away with a little smile.

"I'm sure Knut will teach you all you need to know," Sabine said.

I bit my lip.

"What is wrong, Hazel?"

"He punished me."

"Ah yes," Sabine sighed. "There is that. The rules of the pack require it."

"And also, it is their nature," Muriel said. "Their dominance, our submission."

"At the abbey, they taught me to obey. To be silent and pleasing, as a woman should." My fingers worried my new gown. "How is it different being a Berserker bride?"

Sabine snorted. "We are not silent. It takes a strong woman to be a Berserker mate."

"I am not very strong."

"It takes great strength to give up your old life for someone, but that is what love is."

I stared at Sabine. She was fierce and brilliant. Muriel was beautiful and strong. These women were powerful enough to each mate with not just one, but two brutal Berserkers.

"There is power in surrender," Sabine said. With the set of her chin, I could not imagine her surrendering at all. Perhaps it took two men to challenge her. "All magic requires sacrifice. Our magic requires a sacrifice of the heart. The more we submit, the more powerful we become."

"The power to heal and to create, not destroy," Muriel said. "In this way, we balance the beast."

"But both require strength," Sabine rose and came to stand before me. "There is strength in leading, and strength in following."

I blew out a breath. "Knut has been a long time alone."

"You will teach him to soften, to love," Muriel said. "In that area, you will lead."

"The abbey taught you lies to force your obedience. We have come to you to give you the truth. If you stay with Knut, there will be times when you must bow to his will. But in the end, everything is done with your consent," Sabine gave me a sharp look that penetrated to my soul. "Do you choose him, Hazel?"

I knew the answer right away. I would speak the truth, even if it frightened me. "I belong to him, as he belongs to me."

Sabine sat back, gave Muriel a knowing nod. "We'll tell the Alphas."

KNUT

The four warriors met me as I left the Alpha's audience. Leif and Brokk, Rolf and Thorbjorn had always been ready to fight at my back, even before the witch cursed us.

"Thank you," I said. They blinked at me in surprise, and I felt ashamed. Had it been so long since I expressed my gratitude, my need for the pack? "Without you, Hazel and I might still be lost."

"You were close to being free of the fog," Thorbjorn, the largest of them, came to throw his arm around me. We pounded each other's backs, until the pack bonds between us hummed.

"I was a fool to stay away," I said. My arrogance put my mate at risk.

"We'd have done the same, if we'd had a chance to catch a mate." Leif cocked his head to the side. "Well? What did the Alphas say?"

"I must speak to Hazel." I'd begged my leaders to punish me for dishonoring the pack. They'd refused, lauding me instead for rescuing and claiming a spaewife. Even my disobedience, they'd forgiven.

I could only hope Hazel would do the same.

"Your mate is waiting for you," Rolf said. He crossed his arms, leaning against a boulder. Slight and slender, he was smaller than most Berserkers and the best tracker. "She is in the lodge we built for you two, while we were waiting for the Alpha's orders."

"What orders?" I asked.

"Did you not hear?" Thorbjorn clapped a hand on my shoulder. "We go to rescue the rest of the women at the abbey. They are all spaewives. The Corpse King collected them there, for his evil purpose."

Leif rubbed his hands together. "Some of them will become our brides."

"You will be excused from the fight, of course," Brokk assured me. "You will be too busy with your mate."

I frowned.

"What's wrong, Knut?" Thorbjorn said. He and Rolf had been studying me and exchanged knowing glances.

"If Hazel was my mate, I would not hesitate to go to her," Leif added and grunted when Brokk elbowed him.

"I lost control." Shame made my voice and chest tight. "She trusted me, and I betrayed her. She lived her life in slavery, at the abbey. I will not force her to stay with me."

"She asked to see you," Leif said.

"Then I will go to her and set her free."

"You are her mate," Brokk crossed his arms over his chest. "You are already bound together."

"I will not risk hurting her again."

"You will not hurt her," Rolf scoffed.

"At least, you won't hurt her in a way she doesn't like. That's what sets these spaewives apart." Leif tossed his dagger up, letting it tumble hilt over blade before catching it and waving it to make his point. "They like some pain."

"They give the beast what it craves," Thorbjorn rumbled. "Surrender."

"She doesn't like it." I grunted.

"She likes you," Leif pointed out.

"She is brave enough to stand up to you?" Brokk asked.

"Aye." I couldn't stop the corner of my mouth tipping up. "She is a little warrior."

"Good," Rolf left the boulder to grip my arm. "She is strong. She can stand up to you and anything the beast gives her."

"She does not want to surrender," I told her. "She fights it."

"So fight back," Leif winked. "And win."

HAZEL

The sisters left me in the lodge. "We will take the guards with us, but do not stray far," they cautioned. "We will send Knut to you."

I wanted to call them back and tell them I had no wish to see him if he did not want me, but I could not.

Though there was a bed piled high with soft pelts, I paced the floor, unable to sleep.

Finally I pushed open the great lodge door and explored my surroundings. The forest had been cut away to make room for the lodge and a clearing around it. A cluster of wildflowers grew near a stump. The giant Berserkers must have carefully cut the tree down, taking care not to crush the delicate blooms. I stooped to pick one and a shadow fell over me.

"Knut!" I sprang up, ready to bounce into his arms, when I saw his solemn face.

"Hazel," He passed a hand over my head, but didn't quite touch me. "You are looking well."

"As are you," I said. Where was the confident warrior, ready to scoop me up and carry me into the lodge?

Knut was studying the structure, so I nodded to it.

"This is the lodge where I am to live. I cannot go back to the abbey."

"No, you cannot."

I twisted my hands in my skirts. "This new life frightens me, but I must accept it."

"You are always the most courageous when you are afraid."

"Knut," I leaned towards him, and he stepped back.

"Hazel, I must apologize."

"For what?"

"For losing control. The Alphas were merciful, otherwise I would not even be able to see you again."

I sucked in a breath.

"I should let you go, Hazel. You deserve a better man. I am a warrior. It is too much to hope that I will be able to soften and love you."

I clenched my hands at my sides to keep from grasping at him. "You told me you would not ever let me go. You said it would be your death."

"I would sacrifice my life for you," he said sadly.

"You cannot go."

"No?"

"No. We are bonded. I hear you in my mind. A bond is for life, is it not?" I had to rely on what Sabine and Muriel told me.

"Yes, it is."

"So you will doom me to die as well." I put my hands on my hips, but he shook his head and turned away. "Surely there is a way for us to be together. Knut...I need you." Running to him, I caught his hand. "In a few nights there is a full moon. My fevers will be strong until then. Perhaps you could help me with them." *When you tied me up, I felt free.*

He blinked and I knew he'd heard my heartfelt thought.

"You could stay until I am out of heat."

"Only until then?" A smile flickered over his face and I knew I'd won.

"Well, after that," I thought furiously, "I need your help here. To grow a garden."

"A garden?" He cupped my cheek. "Hazel, I am an old warrior. I do not know how to handle lovely fragile things."

"I will teach you." I leaned into his palm. "We can tend it together. And you can teach me to fight."

"You already know how to fight."

"Only because I know you are there to protect me." I raised my chin. "I want you and no other. I wasn't sure, at first, but now I will fight to keep you."

"You will?"

I grasped his jerkin and stepped up to him, standing on his boots. I still only came up to mid-chest.

"You will not leave me, Knut. I will do all within my power to make you forgive yourself, and stay."

"You challenge me?"

I tipped up my chin. "Yes."

With a laugh that gusted my hair, he lifted me. "And so the rabbit conquers the wolf."

"I am not a rabbit."

"No, you are not."

With a smile, I knotted my arms around his neck, hitched a leg around his hips and rubbed my sex against him.

His gaze was bright and hot on my face. "Keep that up and I'll have you on your knees serving my cock . I'll spread my seed over your face and touch you until you're hot and ready and leave you like that. See if I won't."

"Mmm," I said, and dropped down again, turning away. "Perhaps I will go into the lodge and take my own pleasure."

I'd gotten only a few steps away before his arms wrapped around me from behind, tugging me back.

"Not so fast. This is mine." His hand covered my mound. "I will tend it day and night and our union will be fruitful."

"Come then, my mate," I purred. "My garden needs plowing."

In an instant, I was up in his arms and Knut was striding to the lodge. I reached out and opened the door for us. He did not stop until he'd laid me on the bed.

He flipped up my skirts, not bothering to strip his breeches before he thrust into my wet heat.

KNUT

I sank my cock to the hilt. The satisfaction on my woman's face told me I should never leave her.

Her legs wound around me. I slammed into her again and again, rocking back onto the bed until I was fully on it. Freeing a hand I gripped her breast through her dress and her pussy spasmed.

"You're wearing too many clothes," I grunted.

"You didn't give me any warning," she panted.

"Nor will I," I pulled out and flipped her over, this time tossing up her skirts to bare her bottom before guiding my way inside. She was so wet, I plowed her from behind, hips slapping her fleshy arse. "I expect you to be naked and ready at all times, my mate. At least for this first month. I told you that from the first."

She arched her back, working against me. I kissed and licked the curve of her ear and whispered my heated intent, "The moon is growing heavy. Soon it will be full and you will be ripe and fertile for me. You will swell with my child."

"Giving orders again?"

"Yes. Make me sons or daughters as strong as you."

Pulling aside the neck of her gown, I nibbled her shoulder. "You like my orders."

"I do not!" She jerked up and crawled away. I grasped her hips and pulled her back.

She yelped as I smacked her bottom with savage satisfaction.

"Knut, stop. I'll be good. I'll be good."

"Kneel on the bed," I ordered. "Arse up, head down."

Quivering, she obeyed. The pink petals of her sex peeked out at me. I squeezed her bottom, and slapped it, making it wobble.

"Knut," she moaned.

"Hush." Leaning in, I touched my tongue to her slick cunt.

With a gasp, she jerked away.

"Be still." I seized her hips and drew her towards me before spanking both her cheeks pink.

"I will train you to obey me, in all things. You will find pleasure in pleasing me." My fingers found her slick folds and teased them.

"Keep your bottom high. Offer yourself to me."

With a little sigh, she did. My little woman displayed, arching her back, straining.

"Beautiful." I parted her bottom cheeks and admired her small back hole. Her breathing picked up. "You have nothing to fear."

"I know," she said softly, into the bedclothes.

I rewarded her with a lick. She moaned, pressing further into the bed. But she did not move.

"Good lass." I stroked her bottom. Soon I would bathe her, and shave her sex so it was bare and smooth, nothing hidden away from me. I would put my mouth on every part of her, tasting and learning. The beast would savor each screaming climax, each breathy cry.

But first I would spank and fuck her until she knew she was mine.

"Spread your legs." I waited until she'd moved her knees as far apart as they would go before burying my face between her legs. Whimpering, she tipped her hips back and pressed her hot little cunt into my mouth.

"Oh, oh." Her body rocked against my face. I added fingers and tongue. Her taste was addictive; I'd never get enough.

"Do not cum until I say," I told her between licks.

Her hands fisted on the pelts.

"Knut, please."

"No, Hazel." I rose up and moved so I could grasp her nape, holding her down while I swatted her bottom again and again. Her eyes were glazed, her mouth lax. So soft and open, a victim of pleasure.

"This is how it will be," I told her. "Your pleasure at my hands. Your life in my care. This is what gives me purpose and peace."

Her small hand drifted up, reaching to stroke my cock. I stopped spanking her and enjoyed her touch while my own fingers played between her folds. A hazy smile crossed her face. From her mouth broke little gasps of pleasure that drove me mad. I waited until I could not take it anymore, and then moved into position behind her.

"Cum for me," I growled, and thrust into her again, pounding her. She braced herself on her hands, slamming back into me with as much force as her little body could muster.

With a howl, I gathered her up in my arms. The beast

within rose to the surface and I scraped my fangs down her shuddering flesh, threatening another bite.

It tipped her over the edge. She screamed, her pussy spasming around my cock as I roared out my own release and spoke into her mind. *My little rabbit. My little warrior. Mine.*

HOPE YOU ENJOYED THIS BOOK! The next books in the Berserker saga are Captured by the Berserkers *and* Kidnapped by the Berserkers, *starring Leif and Brokk, Rolf and Thorbjorn. They are full length, stand alone, MFM menages, no male on male action, just two Berserkers claiming their woman.*

FREE BOOK

WANT MORE BERSERKERS?

These fierce warriors will stop at nothing to claim their mates...

The Berserker Saga

Sold to the Berserkers - – Brenna, Samuel & Daegan
Mated to the Berserkers - – Brenna, Samuel & Daegan
Bred by the Berserkers (FREE novella only available at www.leesavino.com) - – Brenna, Samuel & Daegan
Taken by the Berserkers – Sabine, Ragnvald & Maddox
Given to the Berserkers – Muriel and her mates
Claimed by the Berserkers – Fleur and her mates

Berserker Brides

Rescued by the Berserker – Hazel & Knut
Captured by the Berserkers – Willow, Leif & Brokk
Kidnapped by the Berserkers – Sage, Thorbjorn & Rolf
Bonded to the Berserkers – Laurel, Haakon & Ulf

Berserker Babies – the sisters Brenna, Sabine, Muriel, Fleur
and their mates
Night of the Berserkers – the witch Yseult's story
Owned by the Berserkers – Fern, Dagg & Svein
Tamed by the Berserkers — Sorrel, Thorsteinn & Vik
Mastered by the Berserkers — Juliet, Jarl & Fenrir

Berserker Warriors

Ægir *(formerly titled The Sea Wolf)*
Siebold

ALSO BY LEE SAVINO

Ménage Sci Fi Romance

Draekons (Dragons in Exile) with Lili Zander (ménage alien dragons)

Crashed spaceship. Prison planet. Two big, hulking, bronzed aliens who turn into dragons. The best part? The dragons insist I'm their mate.

Paranormal romance

Bad Boy Alphas with Renee Rose (bad boy werewolves)

Never ever date a werewolf.

Sci fi romance

Draekon Rebel Force with Lili Zander

Start with Draekon Warrior

Tsenturion Warriors with Golden Angel

Start with Alien Captive

Contemporary Romance

Royal Bad Boy

I'm not falling in love with my arrogant, annoying, sex god boss. Nope. No way.

Royally Fake Fiancé

The Duke of New Arcadia has an image problem only a fiancé can fix.

And I'm the lucky lady he's chosen to play Cinderella.

Beauty & The Lumberjacks

After this logging season, I'm giving up sex. For...reasons.

Her Marine Daddy

My hot Marine hero wants me to call him daddy...

Her Dueling Daddies

Two daddies are better than one.

Innocence: dark mafia romance with Stasia Black

I'm the king of the criminal underworld. I always get what I want. And she is my obsession.

Beauty's Beast: a dark romance with Stasia Black

Years ago, Daphne's father stole from me. Now it's time for her to pay her family's debt...with her body.

ABOUT THE AUTHOR

Lee Savino is a USA today bestselling author. She's also a mom and a choco-holic. She's written a bunch of books—all of them are "smexy" romance. Smexy, as in "smart and sexy."

She hopes you liked this book.

Find her at:
www.leesavino.com